A DESPERATE DISGUISE . . .

Quickly, I led my horse into the deserted shadows just beyond the tannery. I dropped the reins over Winter's head and stooped down to scoop up handfuls of mud. He shifted once or twice as I began rubbing the mud onto his coat until Winter's near whiteness was closer to the dirty grey of his mane and tail.

My turn now, I thought, looking around fearfully. I pushed back my hood and reached beneath my cloak. With some difficulty I stripped off the old gown I had worn beneath my wraps. Beneath it I wore the dirty wool and leather clothes Gytha had bought from a boy in the street. I still had Mother's dagger, and I drew the little knife from its sheath, hoping it was sharp enough for the job I had to do now. I raised the knife and, wincing, severed the first few strands of my long hair.

OTHER SPEAK BOOKS YOU MAY ENJOY

FAR TRAVELER

REBECCA TINGLE

speak

An Imprint of Penguin Group (USA) Inc.

SPEAK
Published by the Penguin Group
Penguin Group (USA) Inc.,
345 Hudson Street, New York, New York 10014, U.S.A.
Penguin Group (Canada), 90 Eglinton Avenue East, Suite 700, Toronto,
Ontario, Canada M4P 2Y3 (a division of Pearson Penguin Canada Inc.)
Penguin Books Ltd, 80 Strand, London WC2R 0RL, England
Penguin Ireland, 25 St Stephen's Green, Dublin 2, Ireland
(a division of Penguin Books Ltd)
Penguin Group (Australia), 250 Camberwell Road, Camberwell, Victoria 3124,
Australia (a division of Pearson Australia Group Pty Ltd)
Penguin Books India Pvt Ltd, 11 Community Centre, Panchsheel Park,
New Delhi - 110 017, India
Penguin Group (NZ), Cnr Airborne and Rosedale Roads, Albany, Auckland 1310,
New Zealand (a division of Pearson New Zealand Ltd)
Penguin Books (South Africa) (Pty) Ltd, 24 Sturdee Avenue,
Rosebank, Johannesburg 2196, South Africa

Registered Offices: Penguin Books Ltd, 80 Strand, London WC2R 0RL, England

First published in the United States of America by G. P. Putnam's Sons,
a division of Penguin Young Readers Group, 2005
Published by Speak, an imprint of Penguin Group (USA) Inc., 2006

1 3 5 7 9 10 8 6 4 2

THE LIBRARY OF CONGRESS HAS CATALOGED THE G. P. PUTNAM'S SONS EDITION AS FOLLOWS:
Tingle, Rebecca.
Far traveler / Rebecca Tingle.
p. cm.
Sequel to: The edge on the sword.
Summary: After the death of her mother, Æthelflæd of Mercia, sixteen-year-old
Ælfwyn flees imprisonment by her uncle King Edward and, in the guise
of a youthful bard, plays her part in the resolution of the
tangled political enmities of tenth-century Britain.
[1. Great Britain—History—Anglo-Saxon period, 449–1066—Juvenile fiction.
2. Edward, King of England, d. 924—Juvenile fiction. 3. Anglo-Saxons—Fiction.
4. Mercia (Kingdom)—Fiction. 5. Disguise—Fiction.] I. Title. PZ7.T4888 Far 2005
[Fic]—dc21 2002031765 ISBN 0-399-23890-5

Speak ISBN 0-14-240630-9

Printed in the United States of America

For Afton and Miranda
with all thanks to Kathy
Seo hæfde moncynnes,   mine gefræge,
leohteste hond   lofes to wyrcenne.
—R. T.

NOTE

SOME OF THE NAMES IN THIS STORY ARE TAKEN FROM OLD English, a version of our language spoken more than a thousand years ago. To make these words look more familiar, I have changed the Old English rune letters wyn (ƿ), yogh (ȝ), and thorn (þ) and eth (ð) into the Roman characters w, g, and th. Another letter called æsc (æ) remains, and indicates the short "a" of our word "cat." So the first sound in the name "Ælfwyn" matches the first sound in the better-known name "Alfred." One more detail of Old English pronunciation: The letters "sc" make the "sh" sound. When you see the word *scop* (which means "bard"), remember to read it as "shop."

Ælfwyn's story takes place on the shifting battlefield of tenth-century Britain. Danish invaders have seized land north of the Humber River and have settled there among the English people who were there before them. Raiding parties of Danes and rival Norsemen continue to attack English fortresses close to the northern boundary of Anglo-Saxon territory. Mercia, once the largest and strongest of the English kingdoms, has declined and come into the care of Lady Æthelflæd. She looks to Wessex where her brother, the West Saxon ruler King Edward, has wealth and men enough to help preserve Mercia's Northumbrian border—but this alliance will come with unexpected risks.

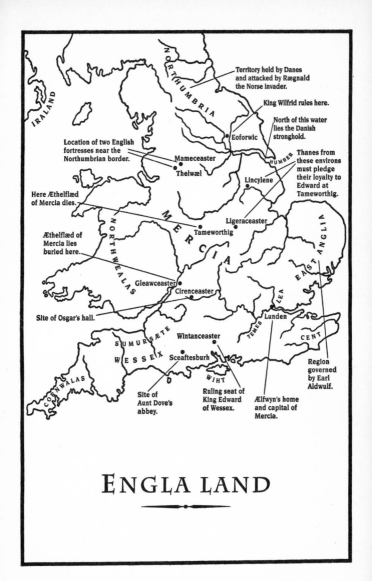

Territory held by Danes and attacked by Rægnald the Norse invader.

King Wilfrid rules here.

North of this water lies the Danish stronghold.

Thanes from these environs must pledge their loyalty to Edward at Tameworthig.

Location of two English fortresses near the Northumbrian border.

Here Æthelflæd of Mercia dies.

Æthelflæd of Mercia lies buried here.

Site of Osgar's hall.

Site of Aunt Dove's abbey.

Ruling seat of King Edward of Wessex.

Ælfwyn's home and capital of Mercia.

Region governed by Earl Aldwulf.

IRALAND

NORTHUMBRIA

Eoforwic

HUMBER

Mameceaster

Thelwæl

Lincylene

NORTHWEALAS

MERCIA

EAST ANGLIA

Tameworthig

Ligeraceaster

Gleawceaster

Cirenceaster

LEA

TEMES

Lunden

CENT

SUMURSÆTE

Wintanceaster

WESSEX

Sceaftesburh

WIHT

CORNWALAS

ENGLA LAND

RAIN BEAT DOWN, WHIPPING ACROSS THE FACE OF THE SOLI-
tary rider. His horse slipped in the mud of the mountain
path, and the man cursed, then bit his tongue. The horse
was all he had left, now that his Lord Alric had gone to his
grave without an heir.

The man raised a dripping hand to shield his eyes from
the rain. Had he seen a light in the dusk ahead of him? Yes,
there it was again—a brief glow that vanished. Above the
odors of sodden earth and wet horse a new smell reached
him: woodsmoke. The man urged his horse forward. There
might be a roof for a homeless traveler tonight, after all.

It was a real settlement, he saw as he passed among the
sturdy, thatched buildings. In the center of the little burgh
stood a tall, fine-timbered hall. One of its large doors
opened, spilling light out into the darkness, along with
sounds of talk and laughter. Warm food, the rider thought,
and drink, and a stable for my horse.

A willing lad took the horse away, and someone showed

him a place on a bench and gave him a bowl of rabbit stew. Farmers, the traveler judged, looking around as he chewed, and craftsmen. There were a few men at the far end of the hall who could only be a nobleman's retainers, with their ring mail and leather armor, their battle-scarred faces. Everything here spoke of prosperity, of a lord who had made a good life for his people. The stranger hunched over his supper. He, too, had once known happiness in a good household.

The traveler sighed, and raised his head warily. These people might ask him for his story now—small payment for their kindness. Nevertheless, it seemed hard to tell of his misfortune in the face of such comfort. The hall was quieter now, and as he looked around, the man saw that the people on the benches around him were turning toward the high table. A strong voice was sounding through the hall, hushing conversation—a woman's voice, the stranger realized, and he craned his neck to see who spoke.

She was sitting in the large carved seat, the place of honor, where the lord might sit with his lady beside him. But there was no lord, only a boy child on her lap who leaned his dark head against her shoulder. The lady had balanced a harp in the crook of her arm, and she reached around the child to touch its strings. Inclining her head toward the notes, she began to sing, her mellow voice reaching past the brightness of the hearth to the dimmest corners of the hall, and floating up toward the smoky roof beams. She sang the story of a captured princess, and then told a tale of separated lovers, filling the room with their grief. When that story was finished, the people called for more, and she began the lament of a scop, a storyteller and singer who had lost the favor of his king.

"Who is she?" the stranger asked the man beside him. He'd meant to speak softly, but his voice echoed across the hall, and the lady heard. She looked up, and the visitor hastily ducked, ashamed to have interrupted the performance.

"A newcomer," the lady said. The man glanced up to find her gazing at him. She wore no noblewoman's circlet, he noticed, only the plaited coils of her light brown hair. But her gown was fine, and she was clearly mistress of this gathering. He cleared his throat.

"My lady," he said haltingly, "I have not heard a woman who, er, I mean, the scops who played for my lord Alric—" He stopped, red-faced, unable to turn his clumsy words into a compliment. The lady smiled.

"Be easy here, and rest yourself." She ran her eyes around the crowd. "Shall I explain why the lady of this burgh does not pass the cup to all her good retainers in noble silence?" The child on her lap laughed, along with many of her listeners, and the man felt an elbow poke him good-naturedly in the ribs. For the first time in many days the lines of worry eased on his face. Someone had filled his cup again, and he took it and drank gratefully.

"Listen! This tale might have happened differently," the lady was beginning, "if I had learned to ride as well as I learned to read. . . ."

I
ÆLFWYN

1

GIFT HORSE

"WE'LL BE LATE!"

"No, we won't. Come on, Ælfwyn!" My cousin Æthelstan grabbed my hand and dragged me along after him. We were nearing the stables, and the morning press of riders, servants, and stable hands jostled around us, drowning out Æthelstan's words.

"But Brother Grimbald is expecting us," I protested. "Remember what happened last time we missed our Latin lesson?"

"On the first day of the spring market?" Æthelstan asked. "That was just ill luck. How could I have known that your mother would be at the armorer's stall as we passed?" My cousin plunged through a stable doorway and led me along the dim corridor between the stalls.

"But I . . ."

"Don't you want to see him again?" Æthelstan tossed over his shoulder. "If I had been given such a horse . . . look! There he is!" He pointed at the next stall. I stopped as Æthel-

stan hurried forward. I could see the big white stallion moving in the dusty shadows, and I took a step back.

Why had *I* been given such a horse, I wondered unhappily. Yesterday my mother, Æthelflæd, had brought him to
me. "He's a fine one," she'd said, smiling as the horse tossed
his head, "a grandson of the matched greys I brought with
me when I came to Lunden from my father's court. I want
you to have him, Ælfwyn." Mother had put the stallion's
lead rope into my reluctant hand, and I had stood there stupidly, wondering if Mother had mistaken me—her shy
daughter—for someone who might have some use for this
animal.

"A beauty," Æthelstan murmured, holding out a handful
of hay to coax the horse nearer. "What will you call him,
Wyn?"

"They told me his name was Winter," I replied. The
horse's head appeared at the opening and I jerked back, startled. Æthelstan shot me a quick look, then a grin split his
handsome, sun-browned face.

"He may be big, Wyn, but he behaves himself. Look." He
grasped Winter's halter and the horse obligingly brought his
head down, gazing calmly at me with one large eye.

"I've never been a good rider—you know that," I said
miserably. The stablemen usually gave me some sleepy old
beast if Mother required me to ride. I always had trouble
just keeping up with the rest of the company. It was enough

to send me scurrying to the library any time a ride seemed likely.

"I'm telling you, he won't be hard to ride. Just watch this." Æthelstan stepped into the stall, took a handful of the horse's mane, and vaulted smoothly onto his back. Winter merely shifted one hoof, adjusting to the new weight. "See? Still as a stone!" Æthelstan said proudly, patting the horse's arched neck.

"Even if my legs were as long as yours, I could never do that." I frowned up at my cousin.

"Here, I'll help you up," Æthelstan said eagerly, leaning down to catch my arm.

"No! I can't!"

But he had already begun to heave me up, and in another moment I was straddling the white warhorse behind Æthelstan, my long undergown bunched around my knees.

"I told you, he's as steady as you could wish," Æthelstan said with satisfaction. "But ease off there, Wyn," he said, craning his neck to look at me. "You'll squeeze the breath out of me."

I made myself loosen my arms around Æthelstan's waist, but my fingers still gripped the belt over his tunic. I had never sat such a tall horse, and the ground seemed a long way off.

"He's been well trained—see how he answers to just a touch here. . . ." Æthelstan pressed gently with one knee, and the horse turned. I squeezed Æthelstan's belt harder. "And let's try this." Æthelstan leaned over the horse's withers and Winter stepped forward out of his stall.

"What are you doing?" I hissed.

"Don't worry, Wyn," Æthelstan replied happily. "We'll just see how he goes!"

No one stopped us as we trotted through the stable yard. After all, I thought as I clung grimly to Æthelstan, Winter was my horse—Mother's gift to me—and everyone in the stable must know that now. Heads turned as we flashed along the road through the center of Lunden, and I muttered a stream of protests into Æthelstan's ear as he lifted the horse into a canter.

"Mother never gave permission . . . miss Latin again . . . Brother Grimbald won't . . . I'm falling!"

Æthelstan heeded nothing but the last words of my harangue, which made him reach back quickly to keep me from pitching sideways. He never slowed the horse, and in a few moments we were at the south gate of Lunden's defensive wall. Æthelstan flung up an arm and shouted to the sentries, who recognized him and called back their greetings. Almost before I knew it, we had ridden outside the *tun*.

I clung in silence to my cousin's torso as he made for a little rise nearby. Winter slowed as we reached the top, coming to a halt as Æthelstan settled his weight squarely on the horse's back.

"Look, Wyn. Isn't it a fine sight?" I gazed out where my

cousin pointed as Winter dipped his nose into the spring grass. Farmed fields lay side by side in strips, their broad furrows barely green with the year's young planting. The road from the gate ran through open pastures down to a distant river, and beyond that lay a tangle of shadowy woodland, dark at the edge of the blue sky. "How could we spend the whole morning in the scriptorium on a day like this?" Æthelstan demanded.

"All this light would make it easier to copy the lesson," I answered stubbornly, but inside I was beginning to feel glad we had come.

It was always like this, I thought to myself. Ever since my cousin had joined our household as a fosterling some seven winters earlier, he had drawn me into his schemes. And yet however reluctantly I went, I always found myself enjoying Æthelstan's company. From the first days of our childhood together, he'd been ready with a smile for me, and with real friendship. Sometimes I wondered why. Wasn't I just the mousy girl who could best him at reading and writing, but who shrank from walks in crowded streets, from the friendly conversation of my mother's many noble visitors, even from the touch of an unfamiliar servant?

Still, somehow Æthelstan liked me. I rested my chin on his shoulder, content. And of course there were things we shared. We were highborn—he the son of the West Saxon ruler King Edward, and I the daughter of Edward's sister Æthelflæd, who ruled the ancient kingdom of Mercia in Edward's name. Æthelstan had rarely seen his parents or his brothers and sisters since he'd come to live with us, and I was my mother's only child. I found myself remembering how in my ninth winter I had watched my father waste away on a sickbed. His death had left me without family except for Mother. And then just a few months after my father's passing, Æthelstan had come, already tall though he had not yet lived through his twelfth winter, often bored with the customs and duties of noble life, and surprisingly fond of his shy cousin Ælfwyn.

"What's that?" Æthelstan asked suddenly. I felt him lean forward to peer into the distance, and the horse, still grazing, took a step down the hill. "Hold there!" Æthelstan slid to the ground and caught Winter's halter. "Good boy." He raised a hand to shade his eyes, still looking out toward the river.

"Do you see something?" I asked, trying to find what had caught his eye. Then at the far edge of the river I saw movement—horsemen, a group of them, with wagons behind. A large party had reached the fording place. I guessed that they would cross the river and be at Lunden's southern gate before the abbey's bells rang to mark the third hour of daylight.

The third hour . . .

"Æthelstan, we have to get back! Brother Grimbald will already have missed us for a quarter of an hour—"

"Grimbald?" Æthelstan shook his head. "It's not he who worries me now. But you're right. We'd best be safely in front of our books when that crowd gathers in your mother's council chamber. Come on." He started to lead Winter down the hill.

"What do you mean? Who are they?" I protested, craning my neck to see the first riders begin splashing across the river.

"I guess you've dulled your eyes with so much reading," Æthelstan said dryly as he pulled himself up behind me—he would make me guide my gift horse back to the stable, it seemed. "Did you not see their crested helmets, the decoration of their horses and wagons?"

I shook my head, too intent on the balance of Winter's rolling strides to look back again.

"It's the West Saxon royal guard, Wyn," he told me, "and my father, the king."

2

King Edward

Brother Grimbald had not finished scolding us when my companion Gytha hurried into the scriptorium.

"Another tardy arrival," the elderly monk said crossly. "Well, Saint Augustine's writings have survived these many hundred winters. They will wait for one more student to find her seat." He gestured to a space at the writing table beside me.

"Pardon, Brother"—Gytha ducked her head politely and tried to smooth her windblown red curls—"but I have not come for the lesson today." Æthelstan raised an eyebrow at me. "Lady Æthelflæd has asked me to bring Ælfwyn and Æthelstan. They are wanted in her council chamber." Æthelstan was grinning outright now, his smile almost a match for Brother Grimbald's scowl. "I apologize, Brother Grimbald," Gytha said as Æthelstan and I stood to go. "The lady said they must come right away."

I touched our tutor's sleeve. "For our next lesson, is there anything to prepare?" The dour expression on Grimbald's face did not change as he ran his finger along the margins, showing me a dozen new pages of reading.

"You didn't have to ask, Wyn," Æthelstan grumbled as we hurried along beside Gytha. "I won't finish half of that. You'll have to tell me what it's about." I grimaced, clutching the book Brother Grimbald had thrust into my hands as we left. I would much rather be on my way to my own room with Saint Augustine for quiet reading than headed off to a crowded council chamber.

"Did you know your father has come, Æthelstan?" Gytha asked. "He and his riders would take no rest, nor any food and drink, before they met with the lady." Her green eyes sparkled. "Their horses are very fine—we should go to the stables after you greet him."

"We've already—" I began, but Æthelstan's elbow in my rib stopped me.

"They've been talking since just before the bells rang for midmorning prayer," Gytha continued, glancing sideways at me, but asking no questions. "They called for the two of you with some haste." Nervously, I caught Gytha's hand, and she squeezed mine back. Gytha had lived ten winters longer than my sixteen, and was a good friend to me. Her sharp-tongued mother, Edith, oversaw all our household affairs, but Gytha would keep our secrets—I knew that, even if Æthelstan did not.

On the threshold of my mother's council chamber we

heard the confusion of voices within. I hesitated, but Æthelstan stepped forward boldly.

"They're waiting, Wyn," Gytha said as she slipped the
book from under my arm and gave me a gentle push into the
room.

Conversation stopped as Æthelstan and I appeared. I
shrank closer to my cousin beneath the scrutiny of so many
strangers' eyes.

"Ah, so you've come." My mother strode across the floor
in her dark gown as men in dusty leather armor and linked
mail parted to let her through. She smiled at me as she
gripped Æthelstan's shoulder and gave it a little shake. "I
wasn't sure if Gytha would find you with Grimbald. Word
reached me that a yellow-haired fellow had ridden off with
my daughter."

I felt my face burning. As usual, Mother had discovered
our mischief. But Æthelstan remained unruffled.

"He's an irresistible horse, Aunt Æthelflæd," he said
boldly, earning a mock scowl from my mother before she
cocked her head (wound round with heavy brown plaits),
and called out:

"Edward, what would you have me do with your boy?
Twice in a month he has abandoned his Latin tutor, taking
Ælfwyn with him. I fear Brother Grimbald won't continue to
teach children who show so little respect."

"I remember at least one cleric who did when we were
young," muttered my uncle as he joined us. He stood even

taller than Æthelstan, and looked as lean as the two shaggy sight hounds that shadowed him. The dogs circled us, touching our hands with their noses.

"It's true that Father John bore your disappearances when we were young," Mother replied thoughtfully.

"And yours," the king shot back. Æthelstan and I stared at the two of them, trying to imagine each of our parents as restless students. "But Æthelflæd," Edward continued, "they are children no longer, as we have been saying."

A shadow crossed Mother's face before she turned briskly to the king's men behind us. "You must eat, and rest a little before you leave us. My thane Benwic"—she gestured toward one of her own retainers—"will show you where to go."

The room emptied quickly, and soon we were left alone with my mother and King Edward. Mother nodded to her two remaining guards, and they stepped outside, closing the heavy wooden doors behind them.

"You've grown, boy," King Edward said to Æthelstan. My cousin stood up straighter, and indeed, he and the king met almost eye to eye. "I've left him in your care longer than some of my counselors liked, Æthelflæd," he told my mother gruffly, "beyond his seventeenth winter, long after many noble sons have learned to ride beside their kin and carry their own swords."

"Æthelstan can ride"—Mother's mouth twisted—"as he proved this morning. And we have given him a sword. . . ."

Her tone was rueful, and I glanced at her sharply. What was happening? Mother turned to Æthelstan. "I hope you have been happy in Lunden," she said in a quiet voice, "for we have been glad to have you in our house-band."

"But now I need you with me," King Edward said. "The northern border is more troubled this season. My retainers and I ride to Mameceaster and Thelwæl to secure the fortresses, and to join any new skirmish we find there." I saw a burst of joyful surprise on Æthelstan's face, and my own heart sank. I had always known Æthelstan's fosterling days in our court would end, yet I had not guessed it would be this sudden.

"My messengers have brought no word of an attack," Mother put in, but Æthelstan clearly had ears only for the king.

"And I'm to go with you? To fight with you?" my cousin exclaimed. His enthusiasm wrung a smile from his father's grave face.

"We hope there will be no fighting, as your aunt's Mercian scouts have reported. Still, it is wise to expect trouble so near the Humber."

My mother nodded in agreement, her mouth pressed into a tight line. Æthelstan was leaning eagerly across the table. I watched him, feeling an aching emptiness grow inside me.

"He has many things to ask you, Edward," Mother said. "Ælfwyn and I will leave you here to talk. I'll have food sent from the kitchens. You want to go soon?"

"Before midday," the king acknowledged. "Thank you, Æthelflæd." He sat down in my mother's carved council seat, and motioned for Æthelstan to seat himself, as well. They were already deep in conversation as Mother drew me from the room.

We stepped blinking into the full sunlight. I hung my head, hoping to hide the tears that stung my eyes.

"Edward is right," Mother said softly after a moment. "Æthelstan has stayed with us beyond his fosterling years. Still, I would keep him longer, if I could." She touched my wrist with a gentle hand. "I'm sorry, Wyn. There's something more I need to tell you."

"What is it?" I asked without looking up at her. My mother stood at least a head above me—she was tall enough to pass as a man when she hid her hair beneath a helmet, and she had learned to ride and carry a sword when she was still a girl. She was always among fighting men, I reflected with growing dread, always riding off to secure the border fortresses she had built with Edward, or to meet with allies who trusted her more than the king. And now she said there was something else. More trouble along the borderlands? Perhaps the Welsh kings were restless again. Mother might ride away as soon as Æthelstan had gone!

Mother took my arm and steered me into the shadows between the great wooden hall and the council chamber we had just left.

"Softly now," she soothed. "Listen to me, Ælfwyn. Your

uncle the king has arranged for Aldwulf, Earl of East Anglia, to visit Lunden. The earl has fought well for the king, and in King Edward's name he holds the lands they took back from the Danes. Now the king looks to repay Aldwulf's loyalty further, to give him an advantage of kinship.... Do you follow my meaning?"

"You're not going away?" I asked in a small voice, and she shook her head.

"No, Wyn. Aldwulf is coming here, to Lunden. He's coming to see you."

"Me? Why would he . . ." Suddenly, I realized what Mother had been trying to say. Aldwulf was coming at the king's behest to meet King Edward's niece, a bride who could bind Aldwulf to the king's own family in marriage. He was coming to take me as his wife.

I couldn't breathe. I jerked away, but Mother caught me and pulled me into her embrace.

"Wyn, don't," she said quietly, her strong arms holding me.

"I don't want to leave Lunden," I choked. "I don't want to leave you!"

"I know," she murmured, pressing her cheek against my hair, "but we will do as the king wishes. We will greet Aldwulf as our honored guest when he comes."

I scarcely remember making my way to the stable, but I was standing outside Winter's stall when Æthelstan found me. The big horse was asleep, one hoof cocked, head drooping until his soft lips touched the straw.

"Anyone would think he'd been pulling a plow all morning," my cousin said, touching my shoulder.

"Has your father brought you a warhorse of your own to ride away?" I asked dully.

"I . . . I'm sorry to leave you, Wyn"—he faltered, letting his hand fall to his side—"but it's right for me to go, I think. It's time."

"And it's time for me to marry, the king says," I said with a shrug.

"Marry?" Æthelstan stared. "Marry whom?"

"Aldwulf of East Anglia," I replied, feeling sick as I said the name.

"He's an old man!" my cousin exclaimed. "Older than my father! And you . . ."

"I've passed my sixteenth winter," I muttered, gazing at my horse. "I'm older than my mother was when Grandfather Alfred gave her away."

"But Wyn, I thought—" Æthelstan gripped the low door of the stall. "It was better to leave thinking that you would be here, in Lunden, when I returned."

"Perhaps we'll meet in East Anglia," I said, looking straight ahead. "I'm sure King Edward's son would be a welcome guest in Aldwulf's household."

"Æthelstan!" The shout rang out down the passageway, and Winter lifted his head, blinking a dark eye at us.

"They've already gathered all my things," Æthelstan said helplessly. "I have to go." He glanced once more into the stall. "You will ride him when I've gone, won't you?" I shrugged, unable to speak, and then his arms were around me. His young man's soft beard brushed my face. "God go with you, cousin," he whispered fiercely, "until I see you again."

"We ride, Æthelstan!" came a second shout, making Winter toss his head, and Æthelstan turned and ran for the stable door.

3

ALONE

I REMEMBER THE SPRING RAINS AFTER ÆTHELSTAN LEFT—A grey month when we rarely saw the sun, and the men who worked the land shook their heads and spoke of flooded furrows and seedlings washed away. Grimbald taught me on my own, or occasionally with Gytha when she found time to read with us. He seemed surprised at the number of pages I wanted to study each day, but there was little else for me to do between lessons. It was muddy in the streets of Lunden, and I had little taste for any excursion now that Æthelstan was gone.

My own chamber seemed best on days when I was not wanted at the library. Gytha saw how I preferred things, and on dim mornings when we had to close the wooden shutters against the rain, she made the serving women bring me extra rushlights and candles for reading, despite their frowns at such a waste.

Sometimes Mother came to read with Grimbald and me.

She had been my first teacher when I was a little girl just learning the shapes of my letters, and her taste for old songs about heroes and their brave deeds helped form my own love for English poetry. Grimbald had little use for monsters and battle-stories, but when Lady Æthelflæd appeared at the scriptorium for a third day, he again put our studies aside to indulge her.

"Save the lines you have prepared until tomorrow," he told me grudgingly. "Today we will read the deed of Judith, a maiden who saved God's people from the barbarian sword." I closed my book, glancing at my mother, who wore a broad smile.

"Your teacher remembers the sort of tale I liked, when he and I used to study together," she murmured as Grimbald turned away to his pile of manuscripts.

"He taught you?" I whispered, surprised.

"When first I came to Mercia"—she nodded—"when he was a younger monk, not long at the abbey. He was gloomy, even then."

My teacher turned back to us. "Smiling, are you?" Grimbald scowled at me. "Well, I don't suppose you know this text." He placed an open book before me with a thump and I shook my head.

"I have heard others tell of Judith, from God's holy writings," I told him, "but I have not read the story myself."

"Good," he grunted. "You can show us how well you read Latin by sight."

It was not a particularly difficult passage. I began reading aloud slowly, stopping whenever Grimbald or Mother wished to take a few lines. I soon found myself gripped by its story of the Jews, besieged by their profane enemies the Assyrians. The pagan leader Holofernes demanded a beautiful Jewish widow, Judith, as a human spoil of war, and the beleaguered Jews let her go to him.

" 'And when Holofernes's soldiers brought the woman to his tent,' " I read, " 'she found the man drunk with wine, so that he fell down beside her in a deep sleep. And Judith stood up, and raised the idol-worshiper's own sword, and cut off his head.' " I looked at Mother, startled. "She did it herself?" I said incredulously.

"Is it hard to believe that a woman could do such a thing?" Mother asked. I quickly lowered my eyes, abashed. Mother had fought when she was still a girl. Raiders had attacked the party that brought her to Mercia, and she had fought back from horseback, and had even killed the enemy leader with her dagger.

"I—I was thinking of the heft of a grown man's sword," I said hesitantly. I had seen enough of Æthelstan's practice with weapons to guess how much the metal would weigh. "And the force needed to sever a thick-necked warrior's head . . ."

"The arm of God was with her," Grimbald said severely,

and Mother and I looked at each other, chastened and a little amused. "Read on, girl," the monk commanded, tapping an impatient finger on the page in front of me. "She kills him, and then?"

" 'Then Judith crept among the tents of the sleeping enemy until she reached the city. She entered, and told the Jews what she had done, urging them to fall upon their foes. In God's name she called her people to battle, and—' "

"My lady!" Gytha burst breathlessly into the room. "Lady Æthelflæd! A messenger of King Edward has been seen riding up to the north gate. He will have passed the sentries by now. I came to find you as soon as we heard!"

Mother stood up quickly. "Please excuse me, Brother Grimbald," she said, shaking out the folds of her gown. "And Wyn, I'm sorry to go," she told me, laying her hand lightly on my head. "Judith is a favorite of mine—her story would make a fine song, I've always thought."

Grimbald bristled, but before he could make any retort, Mother had gone. Gytha followed her, casting a hurried smile in my direction as she went out the door.

With a sigh I turned back to my text, but Grimbald closed the book.

"Enough of Judith for now," he said, and I thought with surprise that I heard a hint of regret in his voice. "Show me the epistle I set for your translation." I reached again for the pages I had brought, but my mind was already slipping away from the writing table and Grimbald's books, following my mother to her council chamber, wondering what message she would receive from the king.

It was not long before I found out. I had barely reached my own rooms after Grimbald's lesson when Gytha appeared again, this time to fetch me.

"Dunstan is with Lady Æthelflæd," she told me in an undertone as we hurried into the street again. Dunstan was the leader of my mother's personal guard, and in the years since my father's death he had become one of the lady's most trusted friends. "And my mother is there, too," Gytha added. I felt myself stiffen. Gytha's mother, Edith, manager of all our household affairs, and Dunstan together in the council chamber signaled serious dealings, indeed.

It was still a shock to find Edith already securing the fastenings of Mother's leather traveling armor. "I must ride out this hour, Wyn," Mother said apologetically when she saw my stricken face. "I ride to Tameworthig, at King Edward's request, to take pledges of loyalty from the thanes of those parts. The king worries that, left alone, the landowners there may . . ." She broke off, grasping my hands. "No, Wyn, don't look that way! Tameworthig is only two days' ride from here, and we expect no trouble. I would wear a mail shirt if we did, not this." She tapped the molded leather on her torso.

"It's true, Ælfwyn," Edith put in, dropping a woolen tunic over my mother's head. "Gytha will stay in Lunden with you, and I will be here, as usual, to see that no one comes to mischief. . . ."

I looked away miserably. Obviously Edith had not noticed how little mischief I got into without Æthelstan to lead me to it.

"My lady." Dunstan stepped forward, straight and powerfully built despite his greying head. "The rest of the king's message—do not forget to tell her."

I felt a creeping dread. What other news had the king sent?

"Yes, Wyn." Mother drew me down beside her as she sat to pull on boots. "You will not find yourself much alone in the little time I am gone. Earl Aldwulf of East Anglia will arrive in three days' time, and you will receive him in all honor, yes?" She cupped my reddening cheek in her hand. "You will be the lady of this household while I am gone," she reminded me gently.

"She's old enough to greet a visitor, and more," Edith snapped, holding out a leather helmet to replace Mother's wimple. "All that time with Grimbald and his dusty books makes her too shy. Should she not go with you sometimes, Lady? Should she not travel to Tameworthig, to let the people see their lady's child?"

"Enough, Edith," said Mother a little sharply. "Ælfwyn does what I ask of her, and will do what the king has asked," she added in an undertone, meeting my eye. I swallowed and nodded.

Mother turned back to Dunstan. "You said you know Aldwulf?"

"By his reputation," the soldier grunted. "I've heard how he took back land from the Danes in East Anglia. Hard-fought battles, they say."

"And now he must rebuild the East Anglian fortresses, and help the folk there plant crops, as we have done so many times along our own northern borderlands." Mother shook her head. "That's difficult work."

"Aldwulf's an old man. I hope he's fit for it." Edith was barely bridling her anger.

"Edith, you don't—" Mother began, but Edith would not be stopped.

"You have not spoken of this to me, but I see and hear enough to guess what is happening. You will give Aldwulf your daughter, at Edward's request," she said furiously. "King Edward will take your heir, will ruin Mercia's future to reward one ally!"

"Quiet!" Mother's command cut through Edith's tirade.

I cowered back against a wall. It was a shock to hear Edith speak this way—to openly call me my mother's heir, although it was true that King Edward had all but let my mother rule Mercia for years.

With a swift motion of her hand Mother sent Dunstan to close the doors. Edith stood, twisting a pair of Mother's riding gloves in her hands. "Do not forget that, like Aldwulf, I am the king's ally," Mother said severely when the doors were shut. "Of course I am also your friend," she continued in a more temperate tone, placing a hand on Edith's shoulder, "and I tell you that I think we can trust my brother. The West Saxon kings have not done so badly by Mercia."

Edith smiled grimly. "It was Mercia's great gain when your father gave you in marriage to his chief aldorman, Ethelred," she admitted, "and Mercia's thanes welcomed your marriage. No wonder," she added with a note of pride, "for your mother, Ealhswith, was a Mercian, born and reared."

"Ealhswith was Edward's mother, too," Mother said in a soft voice.

Edith pursed her lips. "Your father, Alfred, gave a ruler back to Mercia," she repeated stubbornly, "when he let the Mercians choose you for their leader after Ethelred's passing. Now Edward wants to take your heir away."

Mother looked at me and saw how I was trembling. "To be taken, or to be given," she said, and I heard anger mixed with sorrow in her voice, "neither feels just." She took the gloves from Edith, then stooped to look me straight in the eye. "I will be gone for a week, no more," she promised. I squeezed my eyes shut as she kissed first my forehead and then both of my cheeks, the way she had done ever since I was a small girl. With a thudding of boots, she and Dunstan were gone.

"Do you want to go back to your room, Wyn?" Gytha asked, hovering over me. I didn't answer.

"To be taken, or to be given, neither feels just."

Yes, and something else felt nearly as bad: to be left behind, first by Æthelstan, and now by Mother, the people I loved most.

4

MOTHER

IT WAS GYTHA WHO INSISTED THAT WE GO TO THE STABLES.

"Is it true that for two days you haven't even attended your lessons?" she demanded, hands planted on her hips as she stood in my doorway. "Aldwulf is coming tomorrow, Wyn. You can't just hide." She came and crouched beside me where I sat on the bed. "We're going out."

She made me ride Winter, led by a groom on a steady grey gelding. Gytha, no great rider herself, kept careful pace beside us on an old black mare.

"We'll go to the northern wall," she said as the three of us moved sedately along the street. "We can climb to the guardpost and have them show us which way the party from East Anglia will come."

I swayed limply atop my horse. This was not like my last trip on Winter's back, I thought with a pang, remembering Æthelstan's yellow hair blowing around my face. . . .

Suddenly I had to gather up my loose reins as Winter snorted, crowding the gelding in front of him.

"He doesn't like being behind old Scyld here," the stable-man warned, leaning sideways to keep Winter away from the grey's heels. "Knows he could outrun the lot of us."

And leave me sprawled in the dust. "My mother," I muttered to Winter, "gave you to a rider who won't even let you stretch your legs." It was all so useless, I thought with a burst of anger—this beautiful horse, my years of study, the security I'd always felt in our household—how would any of that fit in my life to come?

"Come with me, Ælfwyn," Gytha said, dismounting. We had reached the terraced stone and earth defenses where a changing guard kept constant watch. I slid down from Winter's back and, leaving him with the groom, followed Gytha up the stairs to the guards' shelter.

It was windy atop the wall, and even on this mild day so close to the beginning of summer, I wished for a cloak to shield me from the chill. High clouds rolled across the sky, and I squinted at the shadows they threw across the countryside and tried to follow the guard's gesture.

"There," he told Gytha in answer to her inquiry. "That's the road a party from East Anglia would take." The little ribbon of earth between the fields disappeared over a rise, and I stared at it, thinking about the man who would come that way tomorrow, bringing guards and highborn fighters loyal to him, and perhaps even wagons of fine goods to trade in Lunden, and gifts for the Lady of the Mercians.

And for her daughter—that was how these exchanges

worked, wasn't it? I wondered wretchedly what Aldwulf would do when he found Lady Æthelflæd away, and only her tongue-tied daughter at the Lunden court to greet him.

"What's that?" Gytha's voice broke through my thoughts. She was pointing at something in the northwest, a plume of dust rising from another road, coming closer.

"A rider," pronounced the guard, squinting at the little figure, "alone. He'll kill that horse, the way he's coming!" And indeed, as we watched, the horse stumbled and nearly threw his rider. They were very close now, and when the horse faltered again, the man reined to a halt. Leaping to the ground, he began running for the gate.

"Best get back into the *tun*," the guard told us shortly. "It's Bertwald!" he shouted out to the other guards before we had a chance to begin our descent. I froze. Bertwald was one of the thanes who had gone with Mother to Tameworthig.

"The lady!" I heard Bertwald's hoarse cry. "I need a healer for Lady Æthelflæd! Tell the lady's daughter!"

With a cry I pushed past Gytha and ran down the steps. I reached the gate as the guards helped the exhausted messenger pass through.

"Bring a healer," the man gasped again. "The lady's daughter needs to know."

"Know what?" I clutched at him. "What's happened?"

"Your mother lies ill at Tameworthig," Bertwald choked

out. "Dunstan sent me to fetch her own healer from Lunden. He said you must come to Tameworthig, too."

"Come on, Wyn!" Gytha tore me away from the group and started running toward our horses. After one frozen moment, I pounded after her.

All the rest of that day and through the night our enclosed wagon bumped along rutted roads. An extra pair of horses and two changes of teams in settlements along the way lent us speed, carrying us through the black hours when we normally would have camped. I clung to my wooden bench, shoulders sore from striking against the walls, head aching. Gytha sat beside me, and the healer Dunstan had wanted rode outside with the drivers. Bertwald had only been able to tell us that Mother had taken ill before they reached Tameworthig, and that she lay abed when Dunstan sent him to Lunden.

"He told me to bring you back with no delay," Bertwald had said.

No delay. The sun went down and the wagon got so dark I could no longer see Gytha's worried face. I did not sleep that night. When the light crept into the sky, I climbed out to sit beside the driver.

The sun had passed its midday height when we finally came to Tameworthig. As soon as we had passed the outer walls of the fortress, I jumped down and tried to run. But after the long ride my shaking legs would not hold me. The wagon creaked to a halt and I swayed, clinging to its side as people shouted and came toward us.

"Ælfwyn," a familiar voice said close to my ear, and I felt a mail-clad arm clasp my waist. "Have you not stopped for food or rest?" With effort I looked around to see Dunstan's weathered features. I shook my head, my throat too dry for words. "Come into the guardroom," he said quietly. "There is a little wine." Dunstan began to draw me away from the gathering crowd.

"Mother," I grated.

"Come inside, Ælfwyn." Dunstan was half dragging me now on my useless legs. I dug my fingers into the iron rings of his mail shirt.

"Mother!"

Dunstan stopped. Slowly he eased me down and crouched in front of me.

"The fever took her, girl," he said with grief on his scarred old face.

Silence. The crowd drew up around us—I could feel them come—but I heard no sound from their feet, and the only voice in my ears was Dunstan's. *The fever took her.* Dunstan was still looking at me, trying to see how I would bear the news. "Tomorrow," he said at last, bowing his head, "we will bury her here, at Tameworthig."

Still I could not speak. I stared at him, but the images in my mind were of my mother's ink-stained hands, her quick smile, her slender form in the doorway of my chamber, calling me to a lesson, bidding me sleep peacefully.

"Please," I whispered finally, "where is she."

Dunstan brought me to the entrance of the high-timbered room where Mother lay. Leaving him, I limped across the floor to the empty chair beside the bed. A little breeze made the candle there drip and almost gutter.

I sat down, but when I tried to look at Mother's face, I had to turn away. Her beloved features had suddenly grown strange—I could not find her in them.

"She was riding with us to take the thanes' pledges at Ligeraceaster," Dunstan said dully from behind me. "She was making us laugh, baiting the men who complained of the damp in the marshes. On one winter campaign, she told them, King Alfred himself had to hide in the icy fens wearing rags and begging for food. . . ."

Dunstan shook his head, abandoning the story. "The next day," he finished hoarsely, "before we reached Tameworthig, Lady Æthelflæd took ill with fever and delirium—a sickness from the marsh, some said. . . ." His words trailed off.

"Wyn. Oh, Wyn!"

On the threshold stood Gytha, travel-stained and anxious in the lowering dusk. Dropping the bundle she carried, she came and put her arms around me, but I could not yield to such comfort.

"We should have come faster." I choked out the bitter

words. "Brought her healer more quickly—maybe he could have helped! I should have been here when she ..." *When she died*—I could not bring myself to say it.

"Ælfwyn," Gytha said, touching my face, "your mother—" Her voice caught as she looked at Mother's still form. "You mustn't blame yourself because she's gone." When I did not respond, she held me tighter. "Wyn, you are not to blame."

Blindly, I struggled free of Gytha's embrace. I reached out to take one of Mother's hands, which lay upon her breast. I knew how that hand was callused from the way she gripped her stylus or quill when she wrote, from the reins of her horses, and from the grip of her sword. Now the familiar fingers were cold and still.

Dunstan was muttering to Gytha. "... have to leave her with you ... more riders coming ... by dawn we expect them both ..."

I should have been there when she died. Dear God, Shaper of Heaven, how will I find relief from guilt, from sorrow. ...

Mother's hand lay stiff and quiet in mine, and there was no solace, even in prayer.

5

ANOTHER JOURNEY

"QUIET, BOY. SHE LIES JUST INSIDE."

"I don't think she'll hear. She hasn't slept for two days, Dunstan told me."

I opened my eyes to the dim light of early morning. A thin woolen blanket covered me. *Mother.* I've lost her, I remembered with a rush of sorrow, and I buried my face in the bedding Gytha had laid for me on the floor of Mother's chamber.

". . . not the first time I've heard these reasons of yours, but Ælfwyn is my cousin, your niece! And surely Dunstan will disagree."

I half sat up. I knew that voice—it was Æthelstan, sounding weary and sorrowful.

"Dunstan is a Wessex man, and his lady was our closest ally. His loyalty lies with me."

That was my uncle Edward. The two of them were arguing just outside the wall. I wanted to run to my cousin, but instead I made myself lie still, listening.

"What about Ælfwyn?" Æthelstan responded in a tense whisper. "I doubt that her removal to Wessex will seem right to Dunstan, or to any of the Mercians I know. This is not the best time to speak of Aldwulf and marriage. . . ." Their voices faded as they walked farther on.

Removal to Wessex, and then marriage. This is what would happen to me especially now that Mother was gone. Shakily, I pushed aside the blanket and felt for my shoes.

"All right, Wyn?" Gytha whispered from across the room. "It's the king. And Æthelstan."

"Come for . . . for Mother," was all I could manage. *And to take me away—wasn't that what I'd heard?*

The two of us crept to the doorway and looked out. Not far from our threshold stood the king, still arguing with Æthelstan in a low voice. Æthelstan's hair was longer, his face was browned from his weeks of riding with the king, and his pale eyes looked red. They had ridden through the night, as we had the day before, I guessed. Æthelstan's shoulders sagged. *He will give me whatever comfort he can.* I tried not to think about the discussion I'd overheard, tried to forget the anxious tone of my cousin's words.

"Ælfwyn." The king had seen us, and Æthelstan shut his mouth with a snap. Together they came toward us. "Your mother lies inside, girl?" Uncle Edward asked quietly as Æthelstan clasped my hand in his.

Sadness choked me, and I could only grip my cousin's hand and nod. Edward stepped past me into the room.

For a long moment he stood still, staring at the bier. At last he rubbed a hand over his face and spoke.

"I have come to receive the allegiance of the thanes of Ligeraceaster and Lincylene, as my sister would have done, as well as the pledges of all Mercians at Tameworthig. Afterward we will take Æthelflæd to Gleawceaster for burial at the new minster." He turned to Gytha. "Gather Ælfwyn's things together," he said brusquely. "Tell your wagon driver to harness his horses."

Gleawceaster? But how could she not be buried here in the heart of Mercia? Gleawceaster marked the old border between Mercia and Wessex. My fingers tightened around Æthelstan's.

"Ælfwyn"—King Edward had turned to leave, but he stopped. "Your mother," he pronounced with difficulty, "your mother was . . . she was my . . . I'm sorry." He ducked beneath the lintel and was gone. A tear trickled down my cheek.

"Another journey, Wyn," Gytha said quietly. "We'd better get ready."

6

NEW PLEDGES

BY THE THIRD HOUR OF DAYLIGHT, GYTHA HAD PLAITED UP MY hair, washed my face, and brushed the dust from my clothes as best she could. Now she was packing the few things we had brought from our wagon. Swollen-eyed, I waited outside with Dunstan and watched as one by one, each thane stopped before King Edward, bowed, and exchanged a few words that I could not hear. After his pledge, the thane went with his men to stand behind the king's party. *Mother used to stand and receive the pledges this way.* Many a man she had greeted by name, I remembered, knowing his family's history, and rewarding his loyalty with gifts to show her gratitude. Her gifts to her allies had always been very fine—gold perhaps, a valuable horse, or a beautifully worked saddle.

Sometimes, I remembered, my mother's eye would find me where I watched the procession, and she would smile. . . .

How I needed her! Æthelstan's words stabbed at me again. *Removal to Wessex. Marriage.* Who could help me? I glanced at Dunstan's impassive face, then looked across at

Æthelstan. My cousin looked at me and tried to smile. He had sat with me for more than an hour this morning, speaking quietly of Mother, of how happy he had been during his years in her care. Still, in all that time he made no move to tell me what he knew of the king's plans, and when he went to rejoin the king, I felt more pain, not less. Æthelstan was not the same boy who had ridden away from Lunden not half a season before. He was King Edward's son, and heir to the West Saxon throne.

"Lady Ælfwyn."

I gave a start. Dunstan had turned to me with a little bow. Then he, too, went to stand before the king and it struck me—*The pledge of all Mercians at Tameworthig.* King Edward was demanding a pledge of loyalty even from Dunstan, who had been born in Wessex, and who had served my mother in Mercia ever since her marriage.

So the king must be worried that even *these* men, who had served Lady Æthelflæd for years, might not be loyal to him now.

More Mercian thanes from the land surrounding Tameworthig now passed in front of the king, declaring their loyalty to him and receiving his promise of protection. But I saw some of these men begin to shift with nervousness when the king spoke to them. Others turned their heads anxiously, as if they wished to speak with their companions before their audience with the king ended. The knot of Mercian landholders who had finished making their pledges was growing into a restless crowd, and I could hear raised voices as they milled among each other.

"What's happening?" I asked in a low voice as Dunstan returned to my side. His jaw tightened.

"Girl," he said with surrender in his voice, "I don't want to give you any more sorrow, but I'll tell you what I know." The old fighter drew me up close to him. "These Mercians, who came to show honor to Æthelflæd, have had to pledge loyalty, along with all the levies of their lands, to the West Saxon court. As have my men. Mercian money and goods will go to Wintanceaster now, not to Lunden."

"But Mother always sent Mercian wealth to the king," I protested. Dunstan shook his head.

"Not the whole levy," he muttered, his jaw tight. "Not every silver penny of it, which is what the king will now require." He leaned closer. "These people," he finished in a low voice meant for my ear alone, "these Mercians who came today to honor their lady and her good rule, have begun to fear the end of Mercia itself."

I felt a swell of dread, cold and ugly inside of me. *The end of Mercia?* I searched Dunstan's countenance for outrage or even fear, but saw something far worse: pity.

7

SAINT OSWALD'S BONES

TWO DAYS LATER THEY BURIED MY MOTHER AT THE EAST END OF St. Oswald's Minster in the vast square vault where my father also lay. The abbot began chanting the last words of the Latin service, but I hardly heard him. I stood beside my uncle the king, whose features were as rigid as the carved faces of the saints. Today it was hard to see any clear sign that Edward had cared personally for my mother. But the year the minster was finished, I remembered, Uncle Edward had raided Lincylene to bring Mother the relics of their holy ancestor Saint Oswald of Northumbria. In tribute to Mother's work, Edward had said, Saint Oswald's bones would ever rest at Gleawceaster.

Now the gesture seemed little more than a show of the king's strength, I thought miserably as I stood hunched beside him. The saint's bones proved that Edward would take whatever he wanted—even the body of a holy man—and distribute such possessions where it pleased him. *Am I his possession, as well?*

Not even Gytha was with me now. She had been gone without a word when I had awakened this morning. To whom could I look? On my other side Æthelstan rubbed his jaw as he shot a glance at me, then looked away unhappily. No, I found little comfort in Æthelstan's presence now.

With a grinding heave the monks slid the broad stone slab over the vault. *Mother!* The king strode forward flanked by his guards, and Æthelstan and I followed him past the abbot, past the abbess, and along the line of Mercian nobles who had been permitted inside the chapel for their lady's burial. At the doors the king let his escort go ahead, and then led Æthelstan and me out into the minster's courtyard.

Rain was falling on the crowd of Gleawceaster townspeople and other Mercians who had gathered from the surrounding burghs and countryside. The crowd seemed restless—they jostled each other, and a few began to shove against the royal attendants near me. I heard a shout, and then another, closer this time. All at once a figure in a muddy cloak and hood pushed past the guards and lunged at me, grabbing my arm.

"They buried the lady without me!" the person wailed. "Why was I turned away?" With a cry of panic I tried to pull free. Æthelstan raised his hand to cuff back my assailant when, suddenly, I recognized the stranger.

"Don't touch her!" I shrieked, blocking my cousin's blow. Still clinging to my clothes, the figure slipped weakly to the ground. I knelt and pushed back the hood of the cloak.

It was Edith. But the neat, sharp-tongued Edith I knew appeared completely undone. Her greying hair had fallen down around her shoulders and stuck to her cheeks in wet hanks.

"They buried her without me," she moaned again. "They would not let me in." I stared at her in horror. Edith had come all the way from Lunden to Gleawceaster, and no one had even told me she was here.

More shouts were ringing out across the courtyard. It was a woman's voice again. I looked up to see two guards struggling with another cloaked form. I saw a flash of red hair.

"That's Gytha! My companion Gytha!" I cried out. "Let her go!" I saw the guards drop their hands in surprise as I turned back to Edith. A second later Gytha shouldered in beside me, breathing heavily, and took her mother's cold hands in hers.

"I met her outside the minster this morning when I went to get more food," she told me between gasps. "She rode from Lunden to Tameworthig, and then came here without stopping. The guards wouldn't let us come to you."

"What is all this?" King Edward's voice was angry, growing louder as he strode toward us. "Who disrupts us, with no respect for Lady Æthelflæd?" I stood up and half faced my uncle as Gytha helped her mother sit up.

"This . . . this is Edith, mother of my companion Gytha"—I faltered—"and daughter of Red, a thane who gave his life to serve Lady Æthelflæd. She was kept outside by the guards." The king looked at the women behind me, and recognition flashed in his eyes.

"Pardon, Lady," said King Edward to Edith. "I—I knew your father when I was a boy. My guards should not have kept you outside. And this is your daughter? Ælfwyn's companion?" He pointed at my friend. Edith nodded.

The king turned to Gytha: "Take your mother into the abbey. Give her dry clothing, food, and rest. She is our honored guest." With a nod Gytha moved to obey the king. But Edith was already struggling to her feet.

"I will stay with Lady Ælfwyn." Edith's voice was louder and steadier now, though her body still trembled with cold. "Mercia is her home, and mine. We would be ashamed"— her voice echoed across the listening courtyard—"if you were not *our* guests in our own country."

The crowd pressed closer as Edith spoke, and when she had finished, there was a murmur as her words were passed back to those who had not heard. The townspeople had drawn near enough that I could smell the wet wool of their clothes. I could see their faces harden as they heard Edith's words. *Our own country,* she had called Mercia, as if the king had no claim upon it.

Nervously, I looked for the king's guards. They were nowhere near us. Somehow a group of laborers had pushed past them, shoving their way farther between me and the rest of the royal company. Across the sea of bodies, I saw Edward motion furiously to Dunstan, who immediately rode

over to the wall where Edward and his men had been forced.
I noticed that Dunstan's men, also on horseback, were posi-
tioned at regular intervals around the crowd. They seemed to
form a kind of semicircle. Was I mistaken, or had I seen the
members of my mother's guard urge their horses forward a
step or two—all at the same time?

King Edward was speaking rapidly to Dunstan. This Mercian crowd was clearly challenging his authority here.
Æthelstan, standing beside him, had gone white and silent.

Now the king was gazing at me with a kind of calculation
in his eyes. He flung a sharp order at Dunstan, who dismounted and handed his reins to Edward. The king swung up
onto Dunstan's horse and began pushing through the crowd
alone, toward me.

"Ælfwyn," he barked above the din, "my men and I must
return north. We can't stay here in Gleawceaster"—he
looked hard at Edith—"as your *guests*."

Surely with a word he could have driven the crowd off.
But not on the lady's funeral day, I thought with a lump in
my throat. The love and honor my mother had won in her
lifetime still meant something. The king's final words
seemed to prove me right.

"Æthelstan will visit Mercia to bring us news of your
welfare. And I promise you, girl," King Edward finished with
a sentence that was as much threat as promise—"Wessex
will not forget Mercia."

I stared at his fierce face looking down at me, and I nodded.

The king rode to the edge of the crowd, dismounted, and threw the reins to Dunstan. Without a backward glance he left. Æthelstan and the members of the West Saxon royal guard followed.

At my side, Edith was suddenly full of vigor, glaring after the king with her fists planted on her hips. Relief flooded me, and then anguish. I buried my head on her shoulder.

"Edith, I thought the king was going to take me to Wessex," I said into the sodden wool of her cloak. "Why did he leave me here instead?"

"Edward thought Mercia died with Æthelflæd," Edith muttered. "We showed him he was wrong."

8

STRANGERS

MY FRIENDS BROUGHT ME BACK TO LUNDEN, AND FOR NEARLY two months I kept to my chamber, at first only crying and sleeping, and sometimes trying to eat a little of the food Gytha and Edith brought me. It was Grimbald who drew me out at last.

"I won't have her wasting her days like this," he had fumed, speaking to Edith as I huddled beneath the bedclothes. "Seven years I've taught her, at first because it was the lady's wish, but later because Ælfwyn was a fair student." He paused. "In truth, she was one of my best," he continued at last, sounding even angrier. I felt his bony hand on my shoulder as he gave me a little shake. "I'll expect you in the scriptorium tomorrow morning, girl," he said sharply. "Your mother would have wanted it."

Despite his strong words, Grimbald looked a little surprised when I shuffled into the scriptorium the next day. "See that you come before the third hour rings next morning," he said curtly, but there was an unaccustomed gentleness in his manner as he brought the books and arranged them in front of us on the slanted table. I caught my breath as he removed a tiny volume from a battered leather pouch.

"Mother's handbook," I whispered. Grimbald nodded.

"Edith brought it back from Gleawceaster, with the lady's other things. She gave it to me for the abbey library, but I thought perhaps you should keep it for now." My fingers trembled as I touched the plain binding. Mother had always carried her book with her. Inside it she had copied charms, riddles, battlesongs, bits of histories and saints' lives—any favorite readings she wanted to keep close by to read again at her leisure. Grimbald reached around me and opened the book, leafing through it until he found the page he wanted.

"Remember the scop's poem?" he asked. I stiffened, recalling the night a traveling singer had entertained us after supper. Grimbald had been seated nearby that evening. He must have overheard me tell my mother that a scop's entertainment could never be as fine as the poems I'd been learning to read. Then Mother had taken out her handbook.

"She showed me this lament," I mumbled.

"Yes," Grimbald replied, touching the words written in Mother's own hand, "a lament written by a scop."

I read aloud, following Grimbald's finger:

I wish to say something about myself.
That I was a scop dear to my lord—Deor was my

name. For many winters I held this good office, and
had a gracious ruler. But now Heorrenda, a song-
skilled man, has got the landright that was once
given to me. That passed away. So may this.

My voice trailed off. I could read no farther.

"Ælfwyn"—Grimbald's fingers closed over mine—"this will pass, too."

I kept coming to study after that morning. Somehow it was possible to leave my bed, to leave my room, knowing I was going to lessons with Grimbald just as I had for so many years. But in my time away from the classroom, I wondered what would happen to Mercia and to myself. I had never given much attention to the governing of my mother's lands, but I knew she had ruled Mercia with the widespread approval of her people. She had been both just and courageous. She had ridden with her army, sometimes even carrying a sword, which she knew how to use. I could never do what she had done, no matter how much Edith and others hoped I might be my mother's heir. It was only a matter of time before King Edward found his own use for me, and I dreaded the day he would "remember Mercia."

At the height of summer a message did come for me from beyond Mercia, but it was not the summons from King Edward I had been expecting.

A guard brought me the battered piece of parchment, saying that a monk (a Benedictine, they had guessed by his humble dress) had appeared at the north gate asking for the lady's daughter. Thanking and dismissing the guard, I opened the creased page and read:

> *Greetings, child of the lady.*
>
> *A warrior there is in the world, wonderfully born, brought forth brightly from two dumb things. Full strong he is, but a woman may bind him. He serves whomever serves and feeds him fairly, but grimly he rewards those who let him grow up proud.*
>
> *True friends of your mother have news for Mercia's heir.*
>
> *Look north at vespers.*

Wrinkling my brow, I read the note again, and then a third time. Here was a strange, riddling message, one that greeted me in my mother's name. The riddle's first and last lines were written in good Latin, and the rest in English, as if the author knew that Æthelflæd's daughter was something of a scholar, as if the writer could trust me to puzzle out the sense of the words. . . . I folded the note, and went to find Dunstan.

"A night meeting. I don't like it," Edith said as she helped me secure the leather armor Dunstan had said I must wear beneath my tunic.

"Dunstan said he would take me just outside the *tun*," I

responded, "where we will quickly have defenders if we need them."

"But the two of you are going alone?"

"Dunstan says that two riders will likely go unnoticed tonight. They called themselves friends," I added.

"Yes, well, perhaps you will pass through a Lunden gate without much notice, but that won't help if you are set upon outside the walls by these 'friends.' Your mother studied war both in books and from the back of a horse while she was still a girl," snapped Edith, "but you, you scribble and moon about. Reading poetry with Grimbald and my Gytha has not prepared you for fighting." She smoothed my clothes. "You can't even ride well, Ælfwyn."

I hung my head. Edith was saying aloud all the things I had thought myself.

"I can stay on a horse," I muttered. "Maybe I can begin to learn to ride the way my mother did."

"Your mother learned her earliest lessons at the cost of my father's life, and almost at the cost of her own," Edith said sadly. "Take Lady Æthelflæd's dagger with you tonight."

Dunstan's eyes widened when he met me outside the stable.

"You rode Winter?" he said under his breath. "Do you think that pale animal won't turn heads as he goes?"

"There are other white horses in Lunden," I mumbled as

my heart sank. I had screwed up my courage to ride Winter tonight, but I hadn't considered his light coat. With a sigh Dunstan tugged my hood farther over my face and we set off.

"Mmff." I stifled a yelp as the hilt of my mother's knife dug into my side beneath my armor. I shifted in the saddle, trying awkwardly to find the rhythm of Winter's trot. Winter was still too spirited for my poor skills, but I had wanted to bring my mother's gift horse with me. Stupid girl.

We made our way through the streets without attracting particular notice. But the guards at the north gate recognized us, greeted us by name, and waved us through.

"What did I tell you?" Dunstan groused. Nothing was going well so far. But I thought I knew the answer to the riddle, at least.

"Do you see what you thought you might, girl?" Dunstan asked, circling back to ride beside me.

"Not yet." I peered out into the dusky countryside. The breeze that blew across the fields from the river Lea brought the scent of wet earth, and of leaves and straw from the fields.

Dunstan looked back over his shoulder to the wall, which would soon be out of sight if we continued to ride. " 'Look north,' it said," he growled. "If we go much farther we'll be alongside the river, too far from the gate to call for help. I want to take you back, Ælfwyn. Even at this distance, an attack . . ."

"Wait. Look there," I replied in a small voice. Somewhere

out in front of us—nearly at the riverbank, I thought—there was a spark of light. "Please," I said, "that's the place. I know it is."

"It isn't safe." Dunstan shook his head. He was in no trusting mood.

"But the riddle—the answer is there." We had almost reached the riverbank. There, on a patch of earth scraped down to the bare ground, burned a lone campfire. Across the river two riders were descending from a cut in the steep bank. As they got closer I could see that the first man wore a shirt of ring mail, an iron-banded helmet, and a sword. His companion wore no armor and his feet, I saw with surprise, were bare. They stopped their horses in front of us.

"She comes to us on a horse as pale as a dove," said the barefoot man with no prelude. "A good sign." He spoke in a flat northern accent, and I could see now that he wore clerical garb—the rough robe of a monk of low rank. The man's tonsured head glowed in the dusk as he turned to his companion. "Those are her mother's eyes, don't you think? Lighter hair like the father. But brow, eyes, chin . . . yes, Æthelflæd's face."

The other man said nothing, only quieted his horse. He kept his right hand near his sword, I noticed. Dunstan's hand also rested upon his thigh, ready to grip his weapon.

It seemed that it was up to me to speak next. "Fire," I began hesitantly, "I mean, *fire* was the answer to your riddle."

"Indeed," the monk replied with a little bow and a smile on his sun-weathered face. *"The warrior brought forth from two dumb things."*

"Two dumb things—those would be the stone and metal that make a spark," I said in a soft voice, and the monk nodded again from the back of his horse.

"A woman may bind fire—on her hearth, and in her rushlamps and candles," he continued. "And if he grows up too proud, too bright, well"—he pointed at the campfire—"you see how careful we were to keep our fire small."

Dunstan shuffled impatiently. "This game," he said, "I've had enough of it. Why did you call Ælfwyn here?" The monk smiled again.

"Your retainer does not recognize me," he responded, "but I have met Dunstan before." Dunstan's eyes narrowed. "You visited me with Lady Æthelflæd, at Eoforwic . . . ," the cleric prompted. My retainer looked harder at the man's face, then drew in his breath sharply.

"Archbishop!" Hastily, Dunstan dropped his head in a bow of his own. *Archbishop?* I dipped my own head, confused.

"My lord archbishop," I said, resolving to trust Dunstan's eyes, and struggling to compose my thoughts, "welcome to Mercia, welcome to Lunden. Please, come under the roof of my house. We will have a feast in our hall to honor you. . . ."

"It is better," the archbishop replied, "that heaven be our roof tonight, Lady, and that only God, who knows all, should hear our secrets. We have serious matters to discuss," he said as he settled himself on the ground. His guard and Dunstan sat down, too.

"You remember our talk in Eoforwic with Lady Æthelflæd," the archbishop began, "five years back, when we spoke of a threat from Northumbria's northeastern coast? We can now put a name to that enemy. He is called Rægnald—a Norseman who draws nearer to Eoforwic with every skirmish," he said, looking from Dunstan to me. "Rægnald wishes to rule Northumbria, to take the throne at Eoforwic."

The archbishop's thane shifted restlessly, and by the firelight his face showed wounded pride and belligerence. The archbishop went on:

"The present King of Northumbria and his thanes and jarls are prepared to fight, but as your mother knew, my own holdings are sadly diminished after years of fighting and negotiating with the Danes. Lady Æthelflæd built two fortresses to protect her Northumbrian border, and to guard against invasion from the Danes—one at Eddisbury, and one at Runcorn. Just before she died," he said, watching me, "we wrote to her asking for further support for English people north of the Humber. Indeed, we proposed an armed alliance against this Rægnald, who is an enemy of English people and Danes alike. Now she is gone, and we have come to you."

To me? What did he think I could do?

"My mother was the Lady of the Mercians," I replied slowly, "but I have no authority. Edward is the king. It is my uncle who should receive your petition." The thane gave a loud snort, and the archbishop quieted him with the first sharp look I had seen upon his peaceable face.

"Lady Ælfwyn," said the archbishop very carefully, "Northumbria seeks an alliance with Mercia alone, not with Wessex."

"It's no use," the thane interrupted, pulling off his helmet impatiently. "She speaks for Edward already." Surprised, I stared at the man's strong face and saw the muscles of his jaw working angrily beneath his close-cropped black beard. The archbishop laid a warning hand on his shoulder.

"My mother was King Edward's ally and true friend," I said, pulling my cloak closer around me.

"She was," the archbishop replied in a quiet voice, "but we knew her as the ruler of Mercia."

I found myself beginning to feel angry. These men, these two *strangers*, came begging and accusing at once, confusing me. I did not understand them, and I felt sure I could not help them. I stood up.

"You must ask King Edward," I repeated. "Dunstan, we should go."

"Lady Ælfwyn, please hear me!" The thane scrambled to his feet and stepped in front of me. "Please!" He drew a breath, running a hand through his dark hair.

"We English and Danes in Northumbria have learned to live together. The English observe the laws the Danes have laid down. The Danes respect the church, and allow English people a voice in government. The Northumbrian king . . . was born of an English mother and a Danish jarl. Lady Æthelflæd understood the balance we try to keep in Northumbria. She respected it. But King Edward of Wessex"—the thane shook his head—"with his armies and his hunger for new land, cares nothing for any of this. He will swallow up Eoforwic and seize as much of Northumbria for himself as he can if we invite him across our border to fight Rægnald. Maybe the English in Northumbria will benefit from this, but the Danes, who are our neighbors and sometimes our kinsmen? He will take everything they have. Everything theirs will suddenly be his."

A chill went through me. Everything they had. This man could not guess how well I understood such a threat.

I took a deep breath and let it out. "What exactly do you want me to . . ."

"Ælfwyn?"

I twisted in astonishment at the shout. From the shadow of the gate behind us rode my cousin Æthelstan. "*Æthelstan will visit Mercia to bring us news of your welfare. . . .*" Nearly three moons had waxed and waned since King Edward had said those words. My cousin was trotting up to me now.

"Æthelstan," I said weakly. "You've come to Lunden."

"Just arrived," my cousin said with a white smile of greeting. "I rode to the hall to find the meal finished and all of you gone. I looked for you first in your rooms, then your mother's rooms—finally a slave at the stable told me you'd ridden out with Dunstan, and the guard at the gate showed me where you'd gone. Winter shines like a harvest moon, Wyn. You weren't hard to see."

How long had he been watching us? I wondered with sudden dread. I glanced toward Dunstan and the other men— but the strangers were gone. I turned quickly back to my cousin. What had he seen?

"Welcome to Lunden," I said in a small voice.

That night in the hall Æthelstan stretched out his legs toward the fire that burned in the great hearth.

"It's good not to wear boots," he said, flexing his feet in the soft leather shoes we had given him. "There's been no easy living for anyone in my father's army these last months."

"We haven't had news of a battle," Dunstan grunted without turning his head, his eyes reflecting the flames in front of him.

"No, we wouldn't have," Edith said, amused. "Æthelstan has been telling me how all day Edward's men move stone and wood, to finish Lady Æthelflæd's fortresses at Thelwæl and Mameceaster, just as the lady herself planned. Imagine," she snorted, "West Saxon fighting men turned laborers to complete the lady's work!"

Æthelstan looked at me when Edith mentioned Mother, and I lowered my eyes.

"Wyn," my cousin said gently, "you remember how Lady Æthelflæd used to read with us, how she loved English poems?"

"I remember the way she would do all our work for us if we took care not to stop her," Gytha put in from the bench where she sat, rose-hued in the firelight.

Despite my worries, for the first time since Mother had died, I found myself smiling at a memory of her. Æthelstan sighed.

"Tomorrow I ride to the king's winter court at Wintanceaster," he told me. "But Wyn, something is bothering me. I wonder if you can help." Suddenly I felt cold. Æthelstan's eyes glittered, and looking at his face, I realized what a stranger he had become, despite everything we had shared.

"I learned a riddle on my journey," he said, "told by a scop who entertained us one evening. Do you think you could solve that traveling singer's puzzle?" He was smiling at me, but without any warmth.

I forced myself not to look away. "I can try," was all I could think to say.

Æthelstan leaned back in his chair and recited:

*A warrior there is in the world, wonderfully born,
brought forth brightly from two dumb things. Full
strong he is, but a woman may bind him. He serves
whomever serves and feeds him fairly, but grimly he
rewards those who let him grow up proud.*

I tried not to show my shock. Had Æthelstan heard us?
Had he waited at the gate, watching and listening? No, that
would have been too far away, I was sure of it. But the scrap
of parchment bearing the message and the riddle! Where
had I left it?

"Fire," I answered warily. "Fire is 'a warrior . . . brought
forth brightly from two dumb things'—from stone and iron-
backed steel. A woman may bind fire," I added, still trying to
appear calm, "just like Gytha, tending the hearth over there."

"Of course," he said softly. "Fire is the answer. Well done,
Ælfwyn." He stood up, stretching. "But don't I remember,"
he mused as he walked to the great doorway of the hall, "that
the riddles in your mother's lessons sometimes had more
than one solution? Tell me, Wyn, if you think of another."
He walked out.

"Curse you, girl, what did you do with that note?" Dunstan exploded.

"I'm not sure. I never thought—"

"Well, now we know why Æthelstan came looking for us
this evening. At least he doesn't seem to understand the note,

or know who sent it. If the king travels back to Eoforwic un-recognized and keeps quiet, we might still avoid trouble."

"The king?" I echoed him numbly. "What do you mean?"

"The archbishop's companion was Wilfrid, the Northum-brian king."

9

A HYMN OF CÆDMON

" 'ASH CUT,' "—KENELM OF LINCYLENE SCOWLED WITH EF-
fort, trying to repeat his message precisely—" 'fish caught.'
Yes, that's what my father told me to say." The young thane
grinned, relieved that he'd remembered the exact words.

Dunstan glanced at me and snorted. "We asked Cuthwine
if he had ash-wood spears and salt cod to spare," he told
Kenelm. "There's no need to make a secret of numbering
the stores at your father's landhold. You can go, boy."

"Wait! There's something else," Kenelm said earnestly.
"Father says, 'My thirty stand ready.' "

"What . . . what does that mean?" I said nervously.

"It means," said Kenelm, coming even closer and lowering his voice, "that thirty men from our holding will ride to
Eoforwic when you are ready to fight. I am one of them."

I jerked back in alarm. Dunstan seized Kenelm's arm angrily.

"Enough of that! We asked for an account of Cuthwine of
Lincylene's stores. Nothing more."

"But we heard—" A fierce look from Dunstan made Kenelm drop his voice to a whisper. "We heard that Mercia would join Eoforwic against Rægnald in the spring."

Dunstan was fuming. "You should know better than to say so. Tomorrow I will ride back with you to your father's holding and speak with you both"—he gave Kenelm's arm another shake—"about loose talk. Go rest now."

When Kenelm had gone, Dunstan shook his head. "No good can come of such dangerous talk."

"We only asked the landholders to number their stores, like you said." I slumped back in my mother's council chair.

"And the thanes have drawn their own conclusions," Dunstan said worriedly. "If King Edward hears that Mercians are gathering for battle ..."

"But we're not! We don't even know how we'll answer King Wilfrid of Eoforwic yet. A season has passed since Æthelstan came to Lunden, and we've heard nothing from Wessex. Must we still worry that King Edward is watching us?"

"Yes," said Dunstan heavily. "So tomorrow I will go to Lincylene and stop up Cuthwine's and Kenelm's gossiping mouths with salt cod. Back to your books, girl."

Dunstan was only half joking about the fish, I fretted as I ducked out of the council chamber clutching the Latin translation I'd interrupted for Kenelm. I understood these matters little, and liked them even less. But I could not forget the urgent voice of the visitor whom I had not known was Wilfrid, King of Northumbria. *Please hear me, Lady!*

Still, I thought wearily, King Wilfrid had asked for help from the poorest of allies. Even Dunstan wasn't sure what we should do. I shook my head in frustration. What was it that Pope Gregory had longed for in his *Dialogues*? "A scholar's leisure," I muttered to myself as I headed for the library. Time for reading and reflection, away from the cares of this world. That's what I wanted, too.

What happened next came with the sickening swiftness of a hawk stooping to kill a mouse or a sparrow. Perhaps you've seen it happen: with a rustle and a snatch some small living thing disappears, carried off. It's as if it never existed at all.

"Wyn." Gytha appeared at the door of my little room the next morning. I looked up from my worktable and attempted to smile at her. The winter weather was coming on in earnest now, and I was well wrapped against the cold. This would be my first Christmastide without Mother, but I was trying to push away such thoughts, and to bury in constant study my recent worries about Wilfrid of Eoforwic and Uncle Edward.

"I've found a hymn of Cædmon," I told my friend. "Remember? Mother used to say his poems were miracles, gifts of God. Listen, Gytha." I started to read out loud: " 'Now we must praise the heavenly kingdom's Keeper, God's might and His mind's intelligence, the work of . . .' "

"You need to come see this." Gytha seized my arm and pulled me up out of my chair.

"Gytha!" Crossly, I grabbed up the copy of the poem I had been making. "Stop and listen to this, won't you?"

"Ælfwyn, look!" Gytha pushed wide the shutters and drew me to the window. The street was filling with armed men on horseback. Farther off I could hear shouts of surprise that seemed to be coming from the center of the town. "There are foot soldiers filling the marketplace," Gytha said in a stricken voice. "Edward's troops have come in from every city gate. The Lunden guard never thought to stop them."

I looked down at the mounted retainers crowding below my window. Think, I told myself, crumpling the parchment in my hand.

"Find—find your mother. Find Edith!" I stammered at Gytha.

"I'll come back as fast as I can!" Gytha ran from the room.

My head was spinning. King Edward's men were all over Lunden. The king and his thanes were at my door. *Come for me*—I was certain of that. Dunstan had ridden out at dawn with Kenelm. Gytha and Edith would try to help me, but what could they do? My heart was beating so hard, I could feel it in my throat. How could I have been so stupid? I hadn't really believed this would happen!

"Ælfwyn!" A serving man came scurrying down the passage, calling me as he came. "Lady! King Edward commands you to come!"

❖   ❖   ❖

They took me to the council chamber where King Edward had seated himself in my mother's chair with Æthelstan standing beside him. A contingent of West Saxon thanes ranged around the walls of the room. There was a thick smell of leather and horse, and of men's bodies.

"Ælfwyn," the king said, fixing me with his bleak grey stare.

Should I say something? No words would come. I dropped my eyes and saw my plain brown woolen dress, a pair of old scuffed shoes, the edge of the shawl I had thrown over my shoulders because it was a cold day and I had been sitting for a long time reading. What did Edward see? A shabby girl? A traitor?

"It is time," the king spoke deliberately, "for you to come to Wessex, as a guest in our court."

At Gleawceaster they didn't let him take me! From the passageway I heard the shrill sound of a woman's voice raised in argument. Two women's voices—Edith and Gytha. The muffled sounds grew louder, lingering a moment on the other side of the door. Then they began to fade again, with an increasingly urgent pitch to each new burst of complaint. My friends were being led away.

"Uncle, I—"

"What does she have in her hand?" the king asked sharply. Æthelstan strode across the floor and drew from my fingers the crumpled parchment. He straightened the page and squinted at it.

"Nothing more than a few lines of poetry," he began, but Edward shook his head.

"You thought her talk with that Northumbrian messenger would come to nothing, but we've seen otherwise," Edward said. "Messengers from all over Mercia. Thanes arming. Give that to me." Æthelstan gave him the page. The king glanced at it, then quietly leaned down and held its corner to the hearth fire. Trembling, I watched the parchment begin to curl. It sent up a stream of oily smoke as Edward spoke again.

"Some of my men have gone with your serving women to collect your things. You will come with us now."

The king and his retainers swept out of Lunden, with my wagon bumping along in the wake of their company. Edward had commanded that Gytha alone should accompany me, and she and I rode behind drawn curtains. In my drab clothing and muffling cloak I would not have been recognized by people gawking in the streets, even if anyone had chanced to catch a glimpse of me.

"They're bringing Winter," Gytha whispered into my ear. "I saw one of the king's thanes take him from the stable." Of course, I thought bitterly, burying my face in my arms. He was too valuable an animal to be left behind, just like me.

10

WINTANCEASTER

"WHAT WOULD YOU GIVE A FRIEND WHO SAVED YOU FROM DIS-cussing Earl Aldwulf of East Anglia's favorite sow?" I looked up and saw Gytha in the doorway. "Don't answer that," she said tartly. "I have a better question. You told the earl you'd be at the library, but you were nowhere to be seen, so he came to find me. We went to the refectory, the chapter house—Aldwulf was ready to trudge through the nuns' dormitories before I convinced him that you wouldn't have gone there."

"Gytha, I'm sorry."

"I hope you had a nice time hiding in your room"—Gytha stomped across the floor—"and I hope you have a nice time while I'm gone." Gytha lay down on my bed and closed her eyes.

"While you're gone? What are you talking about?"

My friend sat up. "Aldwulf told me that he wanted you to travel back with him to see his lands, and that King Edward had consented."

A chill ran through me. Make me go with dull, grey-headed Aldwulf? But Gytha hadn't finished.

"So I smiled at him and said, 'Ælfwyn's just come to Wintanceaster these three months. She's had a hard time of it. Instead, take *me* to see your landhold, and when we come back I'll tell Ælfwyn all about it.'" She shot me a wry glance. "He said yes."

"Gytha, I . . . I never expected . . ."

"Would you rather have gone?" She asked the question almost wistfully, and for the first time I could see that she was worried about what she had done.

In a rush I crossed the room and caught her in a tight embrace.

Gytha rode out with Aldwulf's party the next day, and King Edward called me to his council room.

"You will miss your friend Gytha," he observed, clearly wishing I had gone with Aldwulf.

I miss everyone, I thought sadly. My mother. Edith. Dunstan. Perhaps Edith had gone back to her own landholding, now that she had no one to care for in Lunden. I still hoped and dreaded Dunstan might ride into the king's *tun* to release me in the name of all Mercians.

"Do you hear any news from Lunden?" Edward asked without warning. I jumped.

You decide whom I may see, I thought resentfully, and

who may talk with me. "No," I muttered, "I have had no word."

"Well, Lunden is peaceful, at least for now," he said. "It's the Mercian borderlands that worry me, with Rægnald in Eoforwic."

Rægnald in Eoforwic. I felt as if someone had struck me a blow.

"You hadn't heard that," Uncle Edward murmured after a moment.

His pleading voice in the darkness. His hand on mine. He had needed my help and no help had come.

"Where is the Northumbrian king, Wilfrid?" My voice had fallen to a whisper.

The king shrugged. "No one knows. But we will hold Mercia's Northumbrian border. My father took these lands back from the Danes, and I won't relinquish them now." He sighed. "Ælfwyn, why do you think I left your mother to rule Mercia after your father's passing?"

"B-Because she was prepared to lead," I stammered. "And—and because the people of Mercia loved her."

"For both of those reasons," the king said quietly, then added, "and because she was loyal to me."

Because she was loyal to me—and Edward worried that I was not, that Mercia was not. I hung my head, helpless and angry. There was no reason to hope for my freedom any longer.

"When Earl Aldwulf comes back," Edward concluded as if following my thoughts, "we will arrange for your marriage. I will not need to see you again until then."

Marriage to Aldwulf, I thought, brushing away furious tears as I rushed along the street, careening around travelers, tradespeople, and servants. I would finally be married to that stolid old retainer, Mercia was Edward's, Eoforwic had fallen, and King Wilfrid was lost or dead. There seemed to be no escape from these things, not even into the studies that had meant freedom while Mother was alive, and forgetfulness after her death. Nothing I could read now would make me forget that I was homeless, nearly friendless, and about to be given as a kind of prize to one of my uncle's allies.

"Hey there! Watch his feet! He'll kick if you come up behind him that way!" a young slave from the stables shouted at me. I'd almost run into the two horses he led. The lighter horse sidestepped nervously, then jerked his lead out of the stableboy's hands. "Hi! Stop that!" he yelled, grabbing for the rope.

I stumbled backward trying to avoid the pale horse's hooves. The horse reared and snorted, and then I saw.

"Winter," I murmured, watching the slave and another man catch the rope and quiet both of the horses.

"This one's new," the boy responded sheepishly to the

angry shouts that rose from the crowd. "Doesn't like Wintanceaster much yet."

That makes two of us, I thought as I stood tear-streaked
in the middle of the road, watching them lead my horse
away.

A Choice

For a week and a half I waited. I could find no pleasure in reading, and so I sat, hollow-eyed and idle, until Aldwulf's party returned.

"Aldwulf's holding is little more than a half-completed burgh, taken from the Danes just two winters back," Gytha said as she entered my room, still wearing her traveling clothes. "Until they rebuild the defensive wall, everyone must gather in Aldwulf's own villa in case of an attack. And the villa is scarcely larger than a farmer's house! So I said to him . . ."

Then she saw my face.

"The king told me I must marry Aldwulf," I said.

"They have to let me come with you," she choked, catching at my hands, "just like at Lunden!"

"Why haven't *you* had to marry?" I asked. My words brought Gytha up short.

"Wyn, I . . ." She searched my face.

"I thought maybe your mother, or mine, or . . . or *some-*

one permitted you to—to live as a single woman, and to remain my companion all these years."

"Wyn, I've been happy to stay with you," she said slowly, "but my birth has kept me unmarried."

"Your birth? But your mother is a widow, with one of the finest estates in Mercia," I retorted, "and you are her only child. You are beautiful, and you would make a husband rich!"

"My mother," Gytha said, speaking with great care, "was a captive of war in her youth, enslaved in the Danelaw. You have never heard this, Ælfwyn?" Dumbly, I shook my head. "Mother was rescued, but she was not alone: She had an infant daughter, me, the child of some Dane who lay with her and then sold her again. It is known in Mercia that I have Danish blood in my veins," Gytha said with a bitter smile, "enemy blood. We own rich lands, as you say, but I am not a suitable match for a highborn man."

"I always thought you had the life you wanted," I said feebly.

"Our family was almost destroyed by the Danes," Gytha explained. "It will die away entirely now, if I cannot marry and bear an heir."

"I'm sorry." I hung my head. "I didn't know."

"Don't be sorry, Wyn," she said in a quiet voice. "King Edward is giving you what I can't have."

My uncle called me to him the next morning—to make our agreement with Aldwulf, I thought for certain as I trudged through the heavy rain to his council chambers. It was not until I'd wiped my dripping face that I saw not Aldwulf, but a woman sitting in the corner behind Edward.

"Ælfwyn, this is Abbess Æthelgifu," the king told me as the woman stood up, tall in her grey robes.

"*Aunt* Æthelgifu," the abbess said firmly, "or Aunt Dove. Æthelflæd always called me Dove."

Æthelgifu? This nun was the first of my mother's two younger sisters, I realized. I had heard how she'd taken holy vows while still a girl, and how she'd become abbess at Sceaftesburh—an unusually young woman at less than forty winters for such responsibility. I'd always been told she never left her abbey.

And yet here she stood in King Edward's council chamber in Wintanceaster.

"Shall I tell her why I'm here, Edward?" she wanted to know. My uncle said nothing. "Ælfwyn"—my aunt stepped forward to take my hand—"I have heard that you will marry Aldwulf of East Anglia. That is an honorable path for Lady Æthelflæd's daughter. But," she said, turning to look at the king, "a woman may also pledge herself to God, and thus bring honor to her kin."

The king tapped a finger to his lips. "As I told you, Aldwulf deserves my thanks and friendship"—he scowled—"and my own daughters are very young. . . ."

"For Aldwulf a promise now might suffice as well as a wife," Aunt Dove put in, a little sadly.

Edward rubbed a hand over his knuckles. "You see how this could cause me great trouble, Æthelgifu?" My aunt merely inclined her head. "Give her the choice, then," he said brusquely, standing up to go. "I'll need to know by tomorrow night."

Could this be true? I couldn't move. Aunt Dove stayed beside me until the king had gone.

"I'm happy to meet you at last, Ælfwyn," Aunt Dove said. "Æthelflæd always wrote so proudly of you. You are a scholar, she said."

"I used to read with her. Now . . . it's difficult."

"I am sorry to hear that, child." She paused. "But don't you have a book with you, in your pocket?"

I had forgotten the handbook, but now I took it out and handed it to my aunt. She opened it and gazed at its first beautifully illuminated page, which had been a gift from their father, King Alfred, to my mother. For several minutes she leafed through the book, and then she closed it gently.

"It seems a worldly thing to me"—Aunt Dove smiled—"mostly full of poems about lost people, from what I saw. But I'm glad you have it with you." Aunt Dove looked into my worried face, then bent to kiss my forehead. "Peace, Ælfwyn, be at peace. I have asked the king to give you a choice."

That afternoon I lay curled on my bed, with Gytha sewing nearby. I was remembering a story Mother had once read to me, an exemplum from the *Dialogues* of Pope Gregory the Great. A greedy nun crept into the abbey garden and gobbled up a lettuce, swallowing a little devil who rested there. The demon made the woman jump and shout, wracking her until a priest arrived to cast the spirit out.

"Poor thing!" I had cried.

"Poor devil, perhaps," Mother had answered with a grin, "but do not pity the woman. She made her choice."

I sighed. Poems about lost people—that's all Aunt Dove had seen this morning. She would not have understood Mother's pleasure in the strange tale of the devil and the lettuce. A worldly thing, she had called the handbook. It was not the sort of reading a nun would do.

"What do you think . . . it would be like," I asked Gytha hesitantly, "to go to Sceaftesburh? To join the sisters there?"

"They follow Saint Benedict's Rule," Gytha said slowly. "Do you remember how Pope Gregory describes it? The followers of the rule own nothing, though they are fed and clothed sufficiently. From the third to the ninth hour they labor with their hands, with calls to prayer and time for godly reading before and after. All things are done in moderation, as Benedict ordered."

Godly reading, I thought, not histories of battles or scops singing out from the page. I'll face fasting, and night vigils, and holy thoughts until I am an old woman, until I am laid in my sanctified grave beside the abbey's sheltering walls.

"We should go find something to eat." I stood up fretfully, peering at the lowering sun. The ninth hour. At

Sceaftesburh they'd be calling me to prayers now. *I should eat and drink as much as I want—as much as I can hold—while I still can.*

"What should I choose?" My question burst out desperately as Gytha and I sat on the storeroom steps, biting into the barley cakes and withered apples we had collected. "What would Mother have wanted?"

"I don't know, Wyn," Gytha said with a helpless shrug. "She always used to tell us to give you time."

Time to read, I thought, fingering the sack that held our food. Time to think and learn. She gave me books, too, of course. And a horse—beautiful, strong Winter, so unsuitable for a poor rider like me. She might have given me several splendid books instead, and I would have loved them. She must have known that.

"Dunstan used to tell me stories about the time when Lady Æthelflæd was a girl in Wessex," Gytha was saying, still trying to answer my question. "She ran away from her father's home and got lost, more than once! She even stole books to take with her. I wasn't to tell you those tales, Dunstan said." Gytha smiled. "But I always did think it was funny, to imagine the Lady of the Mercians doing such things."

That passed away—my mother's childhood willfulness had disappeared by the time I was born, I mused. *"She ran away from her father's home . . . she even stole books to take with her.*" But she had once wanted her freedom, I suddenly understood. Before all her years of loyalty and obedience, before she became leader of Mercia, my mother had simply wanted to choose for herself what to do. She had remembered that, and she'd given me a horse.

"Gytha," I said, grabbing up the bag of bread and apples, "I—I need you to help me get some things."

"You say you want to ride out in this muck, Lady?" The stableman put a hand on Winter's tether, but kept his skeptical gaze on me.

"Just to the minster. The abbess of Sceaftesburh"—I showed him the handbook—"wants this for her scribe to copy before she leaves Wintanceaster. Immediately, they said."

The man hesitated another moment, then went off, grumbling softly. "A ride in this slop'll spoil that grey coat— and hard words from the stablemaster if he's not cleaned up soon as they're back. Don't suppose the lady'll stay around for any of that, with her own clothes covered in mud. . . ." He returned with a saddle and bridle stained with years of use. Would Aunt Dove begin to search for me?

When the slave had finished, he offered his cupped hands, and I let him help me onto Winter's back.

Had he felt the leather leggings I wore beneath my skirt? I forced myself to look him directly in the eye, and cocked my head a little, as if to say, *anything else?*

"Keep his head in, my lady. You're a small one, on that great beast," was all he said.

No one stopped me as I rode through the open doors of the stable. I was well cloaked and hooded, and no one in the king's *tun* knew that Winter had once been Lady Ælfwyn of Mercia's horse.

Just before I reached the marketplace, I awkwardly reined Winter into a side street and slipped off his back. Quickly, I led my horse into the deserted shadows just beyond the tannery, a place most folk avoided thanks to the stench of curing hides. I dropped the reins over Winter's head and stooped down to scoop up handfuls of mud. He shifted once or twice as I began rubbing the mud onto the parts of his coat not already splattered by our short ride—neck, rump, even his face and ears—until Winter's near whiteness was closer to the dirty grey of his mane and tail.

My turn now, I thought, looking around fearfully. No one had yet ventured into this dark, stinking corner of the *tun*.

I pushed back my hood and reached beneath my cloak. With some difficulty I stripped off the old gown I had worn beneath my wraps, wadding it into my satchel along with the handbook. Beneath it I wore the dirty wool and leather clothes Gytha had bought from a boy in the street. I still had Mother's dagger, and I drew the little knife from its sheath, hoping it was sharp enough for the job I had to do now. I raised the knife and, wincing, severed the first few strands of my long hair.

✦ ✦ ✦

In the hall of the little burgh, the lady broke off her tale. She stroked the hair of the child on her lap, who had fallen asleep.

The traveler stirred himself from the place where he sat listening. "It is written in the Mercian Chronicle," he said slowly, "that the winter after Lady Æthelflæd's death, her daughter, Ælfwyn, was bereft of all authority among the Mercians, and taken by King Edward into Wessex. No other mention of Ælfwyn appears in Mercia's Chronicle, nor ever again in any West Saxon history. . . ." His voice trailed away.

The lady smiled. "Yes, but listen, and I will tell you what happened."

II
WIDSITH

12

LOST

"HO THERE! GET OUT OF THE WAY, BOY!"

With a jerk I awoke and found myself standing at the side of the road, leaning against my horse's warm body. Behind me a pair of carts dragged by tired horses were creaking to a halt, and the driver of the first cart was gesturing angrily for me to step aside. The narrow road was hedged closely on either side by a tangle of trees and nettles. I hadn't expected anyone else to come this way.

Now all I wanted was to get out of this man's way without him asking questions, and without anyone looking at my face long enough to remember it. I didn't think I could get back onto Winter without finding something to stand on—a boulder or a log. But I could see no such thing nearby. I would have to go on ahead of them until the track widened enough for me to stand back while the carts passed. I hooked my grimy fingers around Winter's cheek strap and tugged him forward. Behind us the front driver shouted at his team, and the carts began to creak again. Then the creaking stopped, and the man started cursing.

"Boy! Stop!" he shouted. "Hold there!"

I hesitated. I hadn't much liked the look of the man, or the sound of his voice, but to try to run now would raise suspicion, wouldn't it? Anyhow, it was more than likely that the man could catch me, weak as I was. I smeared a muddy hand across my cheek and turned toward the carters again.

One of his lead horses stood with his hind foot cocked up, leg trembling. The driver from the rear cart had come forward to take a look. The man who had spoken to me was running his hands along the horse's limb, scowling.

"Strained himself," I heard him tell the other driver. "We'll be lucky if we can even walk him to the next settlement."

"Can't move this load without a second horse," his partner grunted.

"There's our answer," the first man replied, jerking his head in my direction. "Boy," he called out, "how much for the grey?" A tiny part of me relaxed as I heard his words. A muddy boy and a big grey horse, that's all we were.

Now I had to decide how to answer. "Not selling him," I croaked, dry-throated, then added, "but he'll pull for you, if you'll pay, and let me ride with you." The lead driver looked at me through narrowed eyes.

"How much?"

"Halfpenny," I replied as firmly as I could, guessing what the work might be worth.

"Load's heavy enough already," the man said skeptically. "Likely he can't pull it, and me and you riding in the cart."

"Half a penny," I said again, "and if my horse can't do it, I'll walk."

I didn't have to walk. Winter accepted the harness well, with only a questioning look at me. He went forward with a will, dragging the cart out of the ruts, and we were on our way with only a few plunging steps. The second driver followed us, with the lame horse limping behind, tethered to the back of his cart.

I had wedged myself into a corner by bracing my legs against heavy bags that I thought must be filled with grain, a precious thing in this season. An oiled cloth had been thrown over the cargo to keep out rain, and I pulled a corner of it over my body and Winter's saddle and bridle, which had been thrown into the cart next to me. Rest, and warmth, and dryness—I could have all three for a few more miles' journey. These were things I hadn't experienced since leaving Wintanceaster.

"Boy, your nag does good work in harness," the driver called back to me. "Thirty pence for him."

"Not for sale," I told him again. I closed my eyes, hoping that would end the discussion. I didn't know enough about the price of horses to guess whether the man had tried to flatter or cheat me with his offer, but it didn't make much difference. I was still running, and I needed my mount. Winter wasn't for sale.

The burgh, when we reached it, was little more than a huddle of huts grouped around a tiny stone church. Probably no priest lived here among the villagers. Instead, I guessed, someone would come each week from the nearest abbey to speak God's word to the churls and slaves who lived in these poor houses and worked in the fields around them. I pulled my knees up under my chin. It did not look like a place that would have much to offer a penniless stranger.

But the driver owed me my halfpenny, I reminded myself as we pulled up to a building that smelled of bread and woodsmoke. A baker's hut. Maybe I could even get some food, I thought, my stomach churning with hunger. I'd eaten nothing since I'd finished my handful of dried meat two days ago.

"Ha'pence," I said, holding out my hand to the man. "You can rest your horse here and hire another if you need to. I've got to move on."

Without answering me, the driver jerked the oiled cloth off of the load, heaved a sack to his shoulder, and stumped toward the building.

"I have to leave," I said, louder this time. "I need my money and my horse." The man knocked at the door, waited a moment, then pounded a fist on the shuttered window, rattling the latch.

"Owe you?" he said, still not looking at me. "I'll owe you a beating if you give me any more trouble. You rested your feet in my cart these many miles, didn't you? Now get away from here. Out of my sight!" I jumped back as he swung out to cuff me with his free hand. Then he turned back to the window and pounded on the shutters once more.

What could I do? I was shivering again in the cold. I'd been a fool, and now there was nothing for it but to take my horse and disappear from this burgh as quickly as possible. I ran back to where Winter stood, and began fumbling with the harness straps.

"Hi, hands off there! Get away from my horse," growled the driver's voice behind me. I turned around to see that he had followed me. Now he stood menacingly close with the heavy bag still slung over his shoulder.

"*Your* horse," I repeated, frozen in place.

"Looks like we've been lugging a thief," the man snarled at his partner, who was also coming nearer with a nasty expression on his face. Suddenly the shutters barring the nearby window came open with a crash, and a man's face smudged with flour peered out.

"Come with our grain at last?" he said querulously. "Took you long enough."

The two carters turned around at the sound, and I had a

second to think. A beating was all I was going to get here. Winter shifted in his harness, restless from the shouting. *He was always too much horse for me, anyhow. No one will believe he really belongs to a bedraggled boy.* But he was mine—Mother's gift! Suddenly, I had an idea.

"My lord expects us by tomorrow," I spoke up, raising my voice so that all three of the men would be sure to hear. "He'll send a party of searchers if his favorite battle horse isn't back in our stables by next evening." The two drivers froze, and the man at the window shot me a cool glance.

I watched as the lead driver's eyes roved across Winter's finely muscled body, took in the sleek sides of a well-fed, valuable animal. Then, throwing one more poisonous look at me, he turned and stomped ferociously with his load to the door of the hut, which now stood open. His partner heaved up a sack and did the same.

I wasted no more time watching them unload their goods, but ran to Winter and began tearing at the tethering straps of his harness. When he stood free, I gripped his mane, clucking to him and tugging until I got him close enough to the bed of the cart that I could reach the bridle. Winter stood patiently as I dragged the bridle clumsily over his head and threw the heavy saddle across his back. I tried to tighten and secure the saddle girth as I had seen the stableman do, but I had to dodge the elbows and knees of my evil-tempered driver as he passed back and forth between the cart and the hut, so cinching the girth took several tries. As soon as I felt there was a good chance that the saddle would stay on Winter's back if he moved a few steps, I led him a little way off and resumed my fumbling.

The carters were nearly finished with their job by this time, and in a moment I heard the lead driver cursing, and looked up to see him shifting the harness of his remaining horse so that the horse could pull the empty cart alone. Before I could complete my frantic preparations, the men were sitting behind their horses again, urging them on a course that would have them pass directly in front of me.

They're coming to get me, after all! I pressed my body against Winter's mud- and sweat-stiffened coat, trying to force him back, desperate to move both of us farther from the oncoming carts. Maybe I could scramble up into the saddle, I thought, grabbing for a handhold. But the saddle shifted almost as soon as I put weight on it. I'd fall off if I tried to mount.

The carters had stopped. They were so close I could feel the heat of their horses' breath and bodies. I cringed, expecting the men to jump down and deliver the beating they had promised earlier.

But the men stayed seated. Glowering, the lead driver nodded to the other man, who took out a heavy-bladed knife with one hand, and with the other reached into a pouch at his waist. I put up an arm to shield myself—then a tiny glint caught my eye, and slowly I lowered my guard. The man had taken out a silver penny. As I watched, he placed it on the heavy wooden boards of his seat and pressed his knife-edge across the soft metal. He held up the two pieces, squinting at them. One he put back into the pouch. The other he flung out into the air. I watched it land in the mud near my feet.

"You were well paid by the men you let hire your master's horse. Tell that to your lord," the man snarled.

"And tell him to send someone man enough to ride his nag next time," the lead driver said. Casually, he cleared his throat and spat into the mud inches from where the coin lay. Then he jerked his horse aside and rolled back along the road we had taken.

I didn't move until the creaking of cart wheels had faded into silence. Stiffly, I bent down and picked up the muddy fragment of coin, careful of its sharp edge. It was quite a new penny, showing my uncle Edward's profile. The carter's knife had sliced neatly through the king's neck and half of his crown. Part of Edward's name and the word *REX* were still legible on this side of the coin, and when I turned it over, I could make out the name of the mint-town: *WIN-TANCEASTER*.

As I crouched there I felt the hilt of Mother's dagger digging into my ribs. I hadn't even remembered it was there.

"Paid you for your trouble, did they?" I jumped, half drawing my weapon this time, but it was only the man who had received the grain, and I quickly hid my knife beneath my cloak before he saw it. He was indeed a baker, judging from his flour-smeared face. "They're a bad lot, but we need the grain. It's a hungry time of year."

The scent of new bread twisted my stomach into knots. I nodded, wondering why he was talking to me.

"Did your master never show you how to saddle a horse properly?" the baker asked me, sounding dubious. I could think of no answer this time. "Let me help," the man said to my surprise, stepping past me and reaching for the girth strap. He began to put the saddle to rights, then stood back and looked at his blackened hands. "Dirt under the saddle. That's bad. You shouldn't ride him like that—he'll be sore an hour farther down the road." The man did not look pleased. "Your master's horse needs tending, boy. Don't you see that?"

It was true. Winter needed tending, and I needed rest. A part of me still fearfully resisted the thought of stopping— we were only three days out of Wintanceaster; I wasn't even sure how far we had come, although I thought we'd been traveling north. But then I looked again at patient, dirty Winter, at his crooked saddle, and then at the half-circle of silver in my filthy hand.

"Is there a place we could stay?" I asked, showing him my money.

"Not with me," the man said, but he was still eyeing Winter, and in a moment he spoke again. "If you think your master's horse could do another task, I'll show you a place where someone might let you stay." I must have looked instantly grateful, for the man burst out laughing. "I was going to say, 'and give you something to eat,' before I noticed that we'd already struck a bargain," he said, shaking his head. "Don't worry, boy." He slapped my shoulder as I drooped. "If the horse is up to the job, you'll have bread and shelter both."

What the baker needed was Winter's strong back to carry a load of wheat to the mill on the riverbank. The carters would never travel down the steep bank for fear of breaking a wheel, or even overturning the entire cart, he explained, so it was up to the people who lived in the burgh to bring whatever grain they had. It was a punishing load he bound onto my horse's back: nearly a third of the sacks from one cart. Winter bore it sturdily, however, and together the baker and I carefully walked him down the footpath to the miller's door.

The miller was a tall, silent man with grey-streaked hair and huge, rough hands. He barely spoke as we unloaded the sacks of wheat, though he did grunt a little when he seized two corners of a sack I had begun to lift and found himself carrying most of the load instead of sharing it. After we had moved the grain indoors, the baker haggled for a few minutes over the price of grinding the new flour. He looked satisfied when he set off to climb the footpath back to the burgh, leaving the miller a basket of new bread, in addition to a sack of flour.

I don't know what the baker said to the miller about me,

but after he had gone, the miller heaved off Winter's loose saddle, took the reins, and motioned for me to follow him to the very edge of the river. There he washed my horse until Winter's coat was clean. I was too tired to protest.

Together we rubbed Winter down. Then the still silent miller led me to a little cavelike barn dug into the riverbank. With a nod, he left me alone with Winter, a cow, a big yearling calf, and a few goats.

I made Winter as snug as I could, draping my own cloak over his damp back. Winter had drunk at the river, and in the barn I found a rack of winter hay that still showed a little green goodness in its stems. I threw down an armful and as Winter dropped his head to eat, I pulled down another pile upon which I curled up. I'd watch until the horse was satisfied, then go and ask for food myself.

How had I come to be feeling so safe here, I wondered, when just an hour earlier I'd nearly been robbed and beaten and left helpless in the road? What would I have done? I'd have tried to go back to the king, said a little voice in my head. I'd have crawled to Uncle Edward's doorstep, accepted whatever punishment he gave me, married his choice of husband, or taken holy vows if he wanted, because I'd no longer have believed I could survive on my own. I was still here simply because a baker and a miller had decided to be kind to me.

A large hand woke me, shaking me by the shoulder. I'd been dreaming of King Wilfrid, of his sword-hardened hand gripping mine in the shadows of a Lunden street. When I opened my eyes it was nearly dark, and the miller stood over me.

"I—I gave my horse some of your fodder. I'll pay."

The miller dismissed my words with a wave. "Horse earned his supper. Now come have yours." Still sleep-befuddled, I followed him. I had expected no more than a bed in the stable for the night, and something to eat in the morning before I left, but the taciturn miller took me inside to his own table, where he gave me bread and fresh milk and a little bowl of dried plums. I couldn't stop eating until every scrap was gone. The miller, whose meal lay only partly eaten in front of him, handed his half-round of flat bread to me. This time I forced myself to eat slowly, and the miller watched me, sipping his own bowl of milk.

When we had both finished, the miller took away the bowls. He returned, carrying a rushlamp and a stick of elm-wood. He set the lamp on the table between us, and taking a short knife from his belt, began to strip the bark from the green branch.

"What is it for?" I asked him after the stick was peeled white, and he had squared it and had begun cutting off finger-lengths.

"The mill-works," he replied. "I mended a part today, and I've no pegs left. Best cut these and let them harden before the next mending job." It was the most I'd heard him say—

maybe the darkness had loosened his tongue. In a few moments he spoke again.

"There are better ways to change the color of a white horse than covering him in mud."

My heart began to beat very fast. "The roads were wet. It was a long ride, with him kicking up clods—"

"Not underneath his saddle blanket, he didn't. Someone's hand put mud there, I'd say."

My mouth snapped shut. If the miller had seen through my attempt to disguise Winter, would he also guess that I concealed a girl's body beneath a boy's bulky leather tunic? Could he tell that no hint of a beard grew beneath the grime on my face? I gripped my knees beneath the table, waiting to see what he would say next.

"What you must do is boil acorns in water, and wash your horse with it, then wash him with vinegar, if you can get him to stand still for it. His coat won't show clear white again until the winter hairs grow. We can do it together in the morning, if you like."

After that, the miller bent to his work, and the only sound for many minutes was the scrape of his knife. Gradually, I relaxed. This man had guessed that I had secrets, but he had spoken of them only to offer his help. What made one person act this way toward a stranger, while others behaved as greedily as the two-faced carters?

I wanted to show the miller my gratitude in some way,

however small. The satchel I had carried with me from Wintanceaster was still slung across my chest, and I quietly took it off and began to rummage through my things. I touched the fabric of the dress I had hidden there after leaving the stable. It was made of fine cloth, but what use would the solitary miller have for such a thing? At one edge of the bag I touched the silver halfpenny. The man had already refused my money, and I did need it desperately myself.

Then my hand slid across Mother's handbook. I had not thought about this possession since I pushed it into my satchel in Wintanceaster. Maybe I should give it to the miller, I thought miserably. That would probably be wiser than keeping it, or trying to sell it later. A fine book in a ragged boy's hands would turn far too many heads.

"Can you read, boy?"

I clutched at Mother's book. What harm could come from telling at least one truth to this honest man?

"Yes."

"What's in that book? Stories? Sermons?" Clearly the miller had encountered books before, maybe in the hands of whatever priest administered to the burgh.

"Lots of things," I said at last. "Mostly poems in English." The miller rested his knife on the tabletop. All evening he had spoken to me offhandedly, the way one cautiously approaches a shy animal. Now he looked me straight in the eye.

"We had books here in our burgh, before the Danish raiders came." He dug his knife into the elmwood, not watching his hands work. "At that time the whole burgh was here by the river, all around this place where the mill stands. But Danes came up along the river, some riding, some in stolen boats. They killed our priest, burned the church and the few books in it, took our livestock, took what young men and women they could capture without a death-fight, probably sold them in the Danelaw." The man lowered his gaze to his work. "No thanes reached us in time. We built again—what we could build—up above the river, so we could run next time. The mill had to stay where it was, and I said I'd stay with it. I ran away before. I won't again."

The miller paused, as if all these words had been too much for him. But there was one more thing he wanted to say. "Long time since anyone read in this burgh. Will you read to me, boy?"

I opened the book. *"It's a worldly thing, full of poems about lost people"*—isn't that what Aunt Dove had said? I turned the pages until I found them: a gathering of three elegies. One was the lament of a thane, a wanderer on earth, who had lost his lord, his lands, and his position. The next de-scribed a seafaring man's perilous life.

But it was the third I chose to read aloud that night for the miller. A scop's voice told this poem, a scop who had seen scores of kings and lords, and who had traveled to many more lands than the lines of his brief poem could list.

" 'Widsith spoke forth,' " I said, reading the poem's first words from the page, " 'unlocked his word-hoard.' " *Widsith.* Far Traveler, the name meant. " 'I have been with the Huns, and with the renowned Goths, with the Swedes, the Danes, the Saxons, the Greeks, and with Caesar, who held power over all the empire of Rome.' " The scop's list continued, until scarcely a corner of the earth remained unnamed. Good rulers and gracious queens, brave warriors and entire armies paraded through Widsith's poem, earning his praise. He had been everywhere, seen everything. He had received honor and gifts for his performances: " 'Many people of good repute said they had never heard finer singing,' " I read.

And then came the poem's conclusion: " 'Thus scops are fated to wander. They meet generous people, eager to make a good name for themselves with heroic deeds' "—I paused for emphasis—" 'and gift-giving, folk who appreciate a fine song, and who have as their reward glory, and a good reputation under heaven.' " My words died away in the quiet, lamplit room. Then the miller gave a rumbling laugh, startling me—it was an unexpected sound to be coming from my sober host.

"You're brash," he said to me, and still smiling, he left the table and came back with something pinched between two fingers. Into my palm he dropped a whole silver penny. "For your performance," he said.

"No! I didn't mean ... already your kindness ..."

"Will earn me a good reputation under heaven. The penny's yours, young scop. I appreciate a fine song."

The next morning the sun warmed my right side as Winter and I returned to the road just outside the burgh. Instead of a light grey horse, this morning I rode a dirty-looking buckskin that smelled faintly of vinegar. In my satchel two round loaves of bread and a small cheese tied in sackcloth knocked against my book, and beneath it all nestled my silver penny and halfpenny.

What would Gytha and Edith think of their lady's bookish daughter if they could see me now? Missing them, I wondered whether Gytha had returned to Edith after my escape, if the two of them might both have fled Edith's landhold in Mercia. And Dunstan—had he gone to Eoforwic in the face of King Edward's actions? If so, maybe Dunstan had been with the king when Rægnald attacked. Who could say?

I feared for my loved ones, and for myself. This journey I was taking—was it the right choice?

On the track ahead I saw a little company of ox-drawn wagons and a few folk on foot, taking goods to market, I guessed, or trading along the way to the next settlement. I set my jaw and urged Winter into a fast trot. Somehow I managed to stay in the saddle, and in a few minutes we had caught up with them. I looked them over quickly. These men did not have the greedy look of the carters I'd met. In their wagons were cloth woven by their wives and daughters, baskets and wood carving probably done during the long winter months. They were farmers, I guessed. I swallowed hard, then made myself call out to them, "Can I ride with you?"

The men had seen me coming, and were already talking about me among themselves.

"If your warhorse can walk slowly," one of them called back, "you're welcome. It's not safe to travel alone in these lean times. D'you have a sword, to go along with the horse?"

I blushed. "Just my knife," I replied timidly. After a second's thought, I cleared my throat. Gripping Winter's mane to hide my trembling fingers, I made myself call out to the man again. "I do have a story or two I can tell beside your fire tonight, if it would please you." I could hear the tremor in my voice; I only hoped they couldn't. The man had stopped, staring at me. *What else should I say?* "I—I can sing a little, too."

"A scop!" the man shouted over his shoulder to his companions. "And a fine one, if that horse is anything to judge by," he muttered, nudging the man on the wagon seat next to him. "It must have been a gift from some rich lord who liked how well the fellow sang." Then he grinned at me, a true, welcoming grin. "Aye, ride with us, boy, and tonight we'll hear you sing, and tell a tale."

It had worked. I'd expected them to laugh, at best, or to turn me away with even less kindness. But now they'd asked me to join them!

"What's your name, scop!" another man yelled from the wagon behind us, and everyone listened to hear what I would say.

Lady Æthelflæd's daughter. King Edward's niece. Fugitive. Wanderer. Far traveler.

"Widsith," was my answer.

13

FAR TRAVELER

MY FIRST DAYS ON THE ROAD HAD BEEN MUDDY, COLD, AND miserably damp. Now I learned what traveling in sunny weather meant: my face burned, my leather leggings and tunic became uncomfortably hot, shrinking even closer to my skin as they dried completely, and then stretching out as my sweat softened them again. Although I did not have the full hips and breasts of many women, I still depended on my cloak to shroud my slightly curving figure. But after several sweltering hours, I slipped away, tore a long strip from the hem of the wadded-up gown, and bound my small breasts flat beneath my clothes. "*Wis-sith*"—wise traveler—they called me when I rode up again in cool shirtsleeves, with my cloak rolled and tied to Winter's saddle.

"Here, take this," one of the men said, handing me a woven straw hat. I smiled nervously and put the hat on, tugging it low over my eyes. No one guessed my secret.

On my first evening in the farmers' camp I sat on the ground outside the firelight. The others were eating, but I kept to myself and hoped desperately that no one would re-member my claim to be a storyteller.

"Ho, boy! Widsith!" someone called out. My heart sank as I heard it. "Let's have a tale from our scop." All around the camp other people mumbled encouragement:

"Aye, a tale from the scop."

"Just like a pack of noblemen, we are, traveling with our own singer. . . ."

"Widsith! Where are you, boy?"

They'd make me leave as soon as they heard what I could really do, I was sure of it. They'd throw me out of camp into the dark, where men like those carters would find me again. . . .

But another part of my mind was moving slowly. There was a poem in my stolen book that I'd read last night at the miller's dwelling—another of Aunt Dove's "poems about lost people." How had it begun? "A wanderer on earth—one who had seen hardship, violent foes, the death of loved ones—spoke out . . ." I thought that was the way it went. But there was no time to take out the book and read anything right now, and anyhow, I didn't want the churls to see me reading. Clerics read, not scops. My companions might begin to guess that I had secrets, and I didn't trust a gathering of jovial men to keep quiet about much of anything.

They were still calling out for me. There was no way to get out of the camp, or to hide. With a burst of effort I made myself stand up. I moved into the firelight, and stood there, my heart thudding in my ears. Opening my mouth, I tried to force my tongue to form the words of the poem I remembered.

"A . . . a wanderer . . ."

That was all. No more would come. I could hear my own breath rasping in my throat as I stood there, frozen and mute. These men had been friendly to me all day. Now I waited to see disappointment and anger fill each face turned expectantly toward me. *Say something! They'll leave me in the road to be robbed and used—*

A humming sound started in my chest. It could have been the beginning of a moan or a sob, but then it continued, a low note. Once more I opened my mouth, and I began to sing, "Rest, babe, sleep, babe . . ." It was something Edith had sung to me from as far back as I could remember—a song to quiet the restless limbs of a little child. My voice dropped to a whisper as I finished the song, then stopped.

What was I doing? Singing a lullaby to noisy men who'd asked for entertainment, a tale? I glanced around furtively. Surely my companions were unhappy.

"Sounds like what my mother used to sing over me," I heard one man mutter.

"What my wife sings to our babe," grunted another.

Only the men closest to me had clearly heard the song, but soon a murmur ran through the camp about what I'd done.

"Have you got anything more for us, scop?" someone

called. "Something we didn't hear with mother's milk still in our mouths?"

"Widsith is your name, did you say? Where in your long travels did you hear that song, then, boy? On a journey between your mother's knee and your mother's hearth, I'll swear, creeping on hand and knee!"

These were good-natured jabs, I realized with relief. I'd been holding my breath, and I took in a great lungful of air before I answered as loudly as I could manage, "No, on a journey to the land of sleep."

And they all laughed. They *wanted* me to succeed, I saw from their open, willing expressions. They were ready to enjoy what I could offer. Suddenly I truly wanted to give them something, just as I had with the miller, not because I desired their kindness, but because they'd already been kind, and words were all I had to give in return. I decided to try again when they quieted.

" 'A wanderer on earth—one who had seen hardship, violent foes, the death of loved ones—spoke out . . .' "

The poem I'd chosen described a solitary traveler. Fate had left him alone and wandering. He lamented the things that had passed away. " 'Where has the warhorse gone? The ring-giver? The pleasures of the hall? Alas for the mail-clad fighter, and the glory of the king! Here riches pass away, friends pass away, a man and all his kin pass away, and the whole earth is laid waste.' "

I let my voice die away with the poem's final pronouncement. I wasn't sure if I'd remembered it all perfectly, but it didn't matter. Something had happened to me as I spoke. Beneath my fear, I'd truly felt the things the speaker of the poem described. His story was like my own.

There I stood in the firelight, all my words spent, for the moment not caring what the farmers would say or do. The poet's words had expressed my own feelings so exactly—something I'd never experienced before. The camp was silent except for the crackling of the fire.

"First the land of sleep, now the land of death. Haven't you traveled any place in our own Mercia, Widsith? Like Lunden, maybe?" someone finally spoke out. There were answering guffaws.

Mercia. So I'd crossed out of Wessex some time in the past couple of days.

"We've got ourselves an elf-singer," said a man beside me. "He looks like a beardless boy, but his spirit's old."

"And tired!" someone yelled out.

"And maybe thirsty!" came another voice, and there was laughter all through the camp. Hands grabbed me, patting my shoulders, thumping my back, and pulling me down to a comfortable seat on blankets near the fire. Someone pressed a drink into my hand, and then others gave me food. They were going to let me stay.

Widsith—far traveler. I earned my name during the days that followed. I bumped along in the saddle, fighting with

Winter, who was fit and happy to be out of the stable. He was friskier than in those first rainy days on the road, and wanted to shy at anything that moved at the edge of his sight. I learned from watching the farmers how to rub Winter down at the end of the day: to wash his legs when we stopped near water, to check his feet for sharp pebbles that could catch inside the hoof, and to scrub his sweaty back and neck with grasses or with more cloth secretly stripped from the remnants of my old gown. I even traded an extra song one night for a roughly carved bone comb to help untangle Winter's mane and tail.

I was teaching myself to move and act like a boy. I also tried to cultivate more boldness as I entertained the group. Most unexpectedly, I had begun to earn my keep with my memory. Still afraid to look in my book for stories and songs, I dredged up all sorts of things I remembered from my life so far.

"A warrior there is in the world . . . ," I began, and let my companions puzzle out the archbishop's fire riddle. I told the farmers a story of a hero who slew a dragon, and then died himself—lines from a poem my mother used to quietly recite some nights to Æthelstan and me in our great feasting hall in Lunden. I spoke maxims: wise sayings about the proper patterns of life. I retold exempla, and that story of my mother's about a nun who accidentally swallowed a little devil made even the dourest man in our company smile.

"Hi, Widsith! Dust in your throat tonight?" someone far from the fire yelled when I sang too softly one night.

"Give him a drink!" came another shout, and a sloshing wineskin was passed from hand to hand until it reached me. I poured a swallow of whatever it was—something biting and quick-brewed—into my mouth, coughed as it went down, then continued in a tone somewhere between a shout and a growl.

". . . long had the monster haunted the fens, a bloody outcast . . . then through the mists, like darkness itself, he crept toward the hall . . ."

Every eye and ear in camp was fixed upon me. I learned to speak out, so that the watchman bedding down among the horses could hear my performance as easily as the man beside me. I was becoming a real scop.

Our pace was slow, and though I was still eager to get as far from Wintanceaster as possible, I kept riding with my new companions. My few days alone on the road had taught me the value of being prized and protected as a member of a larger group.

It was almost a fatal mistake, feeling safe with these men. We were following a major road and tended to encounter other travelers each day, so at first I paid little heed to the sound of hoofbeats behind us one afternoon. But Winter began tossing his head, and I realized that two riders were coming at a gallop. I had only enough time to swing Winter around to the side of the road before they came plunging into our company.

"We are messengers," shouted the foremost rider, "from the king's court at Wintanceaster! Have you seen a group of noble riders, one of them a lady on a pale horse?"

"A lady?" the leader of our group asked, puzzled. "Y'mean like the ones who travel shut up in fancy wagons? Never seen the face of such a one on the road. An' I've never known a fine lady to straddle a horse." He spoke sincerely, but some of our men laughed at the thought and the messenger's face darkened.

"We search under King Edward's orders," he said, snapping a gesture to the other rider, who urged his horse into a trot and circled our slow-moving band, eyeing us carefully. "You've kept to this road for how long?" The first man addressed our leader again.

"The last seven nights. Today makes our eighth on the road," the freedman answered him, reining in his horses as the rest of the company creaked to a halt around him. "Haven't seen anyone highborn."

"Have any of you others?" the messenger called, and the churls shook their heads.

"We all come together," someone told him. I held myself still as a statue on Winter's back, wishing he were some shaggy, scrawny nag, knowing I should never have left my wooded route for the open road. Then the words I dreaded rang out: "Except Widsith. He joined us after the river crossing."

The two messengers were at my side in an instant.

"Boy," the spokesman demanded, "where'd you come from?"

I'd say as much truth as I could—that had worked before. "Stayed with the miller at the last settlement," I made myself reply, my chest tight with the terrible risk I was facing.

"And before that?" I could see they were sizing up my mount, suspicion growing in them as they tried to match the fine horse with the ragged horseman. They might not know who I was, but they could see that something was different about me, something wasn't right.

"That's the scop. That's Widsith," the lead farmer's voice broke in. "He's a young 'un, but he's been all over, I expect." The messenger seized my arm, his horse jostling roughly against Winter.

"Where have you been?" he asked, his voice dangerously low. I had to answer him this time. What could I say? My mind careened. *What in all this world under heaven could I say to make him turn aside and let me go?*

And then I knew.

"Before, I was in East Anglia, attending Earl Aldwulf's court."

The messenger's face fell, and he released my arm. "He says he's been in the northeast, with Aldwulf," he said to his companion. "They said the lady wouldn't have gone that way. Let's keep on." And they put their heels to their horses' sides and were gone.

Our leader waited until the dust had settled a little, then clucked to his ox team to start us moving again. Still shaking, I sent Winter forward at a gentle walk.

"Aldwulf give you that horse, boy?"

I jumped at the question, but the driver beside me was looking at us with only mild interest.

"Uh, yes. I—I pleased him with . . . with a tale." I could barely speak. No one could believe I was an accomplished enough performer to win such a rich prize.

"It wasn't for your singing, that's certain." And the men around us laughed. Even I pretended to smile, but my terror did not begin to subside for several hours, and for the next three days I could not stop squinting down the road ahead of us, worrying that the king's searchers would return.

Then I heard the name of the *tun* where we were headed: Cirenceaster. I had seen from the sun that we were still traveling north, and I had tried to figure out how far our pace might be taking us each day, but I had not suspected this. Cirenceaster was even closer to the old border between Mercia and West Saxony than Gleawceaster, where we had buried my mother—I had hoped that we would be well within Mercia by now.

This was a fine place for the fugitive daughter of the Lady of the Mercians to have fled, I thought bitterly, gripping

Winter's reins until he tossed his head in annoyance. Even if there were renegade nobles here who would take me in, and even defend me against the king, weren't such caretakers as likely to use me as to protect me if the king came looking? I ought to be much farther away.

But I still needed to keep myself fed and sheltered, and these farmers would return to their lands in the next day or so. Well, for now, the best thing I could do was to continue to take care of myself. I would keep my new name and boy's clothes, and try not to be noticed. I would try to find a place in Cirenceaster where I could belong, at least until I could afford to travel farther. Ælfwyn of Mercia could not have done it. Widsith might have a chance.

14

WORDS IN THE HALL

AS WE DREW CLOSER AND CLOSER TO CIRENCEASTER, I listened to the churls talk about what they would do here, and how they would return home afterward. They hoped to sell everything they had brought, even the carts they rode in and the oxen who pulled them. Then, if they could find carters driving back toward their burgh, my friends would ask to be taken along at a tiny price. With their plain clothes, and without their wagonloads of goods, they would appear poor enough to drive such a bargain. If all went well, they would bring home almost every penny they had earned, and keep their families prosperous for another year.

"And what will you do, Widsith, my boy?" asked the man driving the wagon nearest to me. I tried to look careless as I answered him:

"Oh, find a wealthy thane, sit in his hall, and tell him the stories I've been telling you."

It was a response I had thought of as I lay rolled in the blanket someone had lent me, my head pillowed on my bundled-up cloak, worrying about what would happen to me when we reached the *tun*. My time with these freemen had given me some confidence in my disguise, and had shown me that, for them at least, I could perform. Although at Cirenceaster I would face a more demanding audience and might even be recognized, I had to eat. And Winter—we could not count on the tender grass he cropped these days to last past harvest time. I would have to feed him, too, come late autumn and winter. And by then surely I would need shelter, and probably new clothes. And so I had little choice. The wagon driver nodded his approval of my plan.

"Osgar's hall is the place you should try. He's a rich lord, and generous to those who please him. He welcomes high-born travelers to his hall once in every seven days' time. When we get to the marketplace, I'll show you the way to his home."

The market at Cirenceaster had the familiar sounds of animals crying out and people calling, and the mingled smells of dung and bread, meat and straw, earth, cheese, leather, beer. The men I had traveled with were soon occupied in deciding where to set up their goods. But the driver who had spoken with me, true to his word, took my shoulder and with his other hand pointed to where a street cut away from the open market.

"If you go down that way, you'll come to a place, larger

and richer than the other buildings. That's where Osgar keeps his household. Travelers of higher birth always look for shelter there, knowing Osgar's table will be heavy with food, and the floor welcoming to those who need a place to spend the night. Good luck, boy," he said, finishing with a clap on my shoulder that made me wince and take my first couple of steps away from him. "We freemen liked your talk and even your singing well enough. Let's see if you can please Lord Osgar."

Osgar's hall loomed at the end of the street, just as the farmer had said. A vaulted roof thatched with new straw stood above great doors of carved wood. But although this was splendid, it was the decoration above the doors that caught my eye. A huge pair of antlers had been hung directly over the entrance, and they were covered with pure gold.

I stood there while Winter lipped the grass at my feet, and I thought hard about what I saw. Osgar must be a very rich thane, indeed. And he must be powerful: Clearly none of the poorer neighbors had made any move to seize the fortune in gold that hung above the hall door, even though I could see no guard posted.

Gaining entrance into the hall proved as easy as asking. A boy from Osgar's stables took Winter's reins, and the steward led me through the whole length of the hall until we reached an empty corner at its opposite end, not far from the high table. Here he told me to sit, back against the wall, until the guests were ready for entertainment. At first I thought the sight of my fine horse had persuaded the steward to let me come to the night's feast. But as I settled myself for a long wait, I realized that my request must be familiar to the people who served at Osgar's table. To them, I was simply one of many scops traveling through Cirenceaster who had stopped at the *tun's* richest hall to try their luck with Lord Osgar and his guests.

Little did they know how terrified I was to find myself in this position so quickly—I needed to find some new words for my performance! I took out my book, thinking that the horns over the hall entrance had reminded me of something inside it. I turned the pages until I found what I wanted, then read and read again, memorizing words until evening fell.

The feast began somewhat later than the simple meals I'd been eating with my traveling farmers. Today had been a warm day, and so even as the hour grew late no fire was set upon the hall's great hearth. Torches and candles had been lit and placed all around to brighten the cavernous feasting place. The tables were scrubbed clean, benches straightened. Household dogs wandered in to nose around the floor and lick at stains from past meals. Serving people began bustling in and out, and Osgar's guests began to arrive.

The first people to come were men who stomped through the doorway in groups of five, seven, even as many as a dozen. They shouted and laughed among themselves, and occasionally hailed members of other groups with a friendly greeting.

When at least thirty men had seated themselves around the hall, Osgar arrived surrounded by another group of richly dressed people, including several noblewomen. He was a person of average height and build, his brown hair was streaked here and there with grey, and he said little to the folk around him, only nodding at the guests as he passed each table. When he sat down in the central carved chair, however, I saw him catch the eye of the steward hovering near the entrance. The steward disappeared immediately, and seconds later serving people began carrying food into the hall.

It was a fine meal, generous in portions, if not as richly prepared as some of the feasts I had attended at my mother's Lunden court or at Wintanceaster. Clearly many of tonight's guests were travelers who had not eaten nearly so well during their time on the road. Fingers broke bread eagerly, teeth tore into meat, and horns and bowls and flagons of drink sloshed in almost every hand.

I was hungry, of course. Hunger had become the force that drove me into the lives of strangers ever since the rainy afternoon when I'd left the king's court. And so I ate what the busy serving people placed in my hands, but my mind raced away, worrying about the performance that Osgar would shortly require from me, wondering if my plan would work.

With horror I suddenly felt tears start prickling at the corners of my eyes. No scop in our hall at Lunden had ever *cried*—not before the performance, anyhow. The scop's task was to move his listeners to emotion, not to be overcome himself. Frightened that I really would cry, I pinched myself through my leather leggings as hard as I could, trying to make that new pain drive away the old ache of missing Mother, and Lunden—the home to which I could never return.

"Boy." It was the steward standing beside me, pulling me to my feet with a firm hand on my arm. "My master wants to hear you now. Stand there, just below the high table." The man pointed to the place being cleared by servants. "And you can leave your bag with me," he said, lifting the strap of the satchel from my shoulder. I had to let him take it, though if he were anything less than an honest man, I would not see my money again. "Good luck, child," the steward concluded, a hint of kindness creeping into his tone for the first time. Maybe he noticed how miserable I looked. "I hope you please Lord Osgar's guests."

Empty-handed, I walked along the aisle between the tables of feasters, trying to hold up my head. All these people saw me for what I was—a dirty girl in stolen clothes about to pretend she was a poet. But I had no choice if I wanted to survive. Gradually the din of conversation died down as people noticed me coming forward. In front of the high table I stopped and bowed to Osgar and his lady. *Widsith. I'm not Ælfwyn, I'm Widsith. And I have an idea about what would please the lord of this feast, remember?* Clasping my hands tightly behind me, I began to speak.

" 'Widsith spoke forth, unlocked his word-hoard.' " I swallowed before I said the poem's next words: " 'Often in the hall, he accepted splendid treasure.' " It was brash to speak of a reward so early in my performance. *But a scop must be bold.* I swallowed again, and then just as I had done with the miller, I recited the poem's long list of nations and rulers—Greeks, Huns, Goths, Burgundians, Finns, Jutes, Danes—I had to squeeze my eyes shut to remember all of them. Alexander, Attila, Caesar—the people in this room were of noble birth, and many were fighting men. They would be interested in my poem's allusions to powerful folk, wouldn't they?

I'd reached the lines that had convinced me that this was the right poem for tonight. " 'Hrothwulf and Hrothgar kept peace together after they gained victory over the invading horde, hewed them down at Heorot.' " Heorot was a famous hall, described elsewhere in poetry as a very rich place with golden ornaments. I stole a glance at Osgar to see how he received the words. The name Heorot meant "hart"—it suggested the kind of stag-horn decorations I had seen over Osgar's own hall entrance.

Would Osgar have heard the name? Would he know Heorot's reputation as a grand building? Would he see how I was trying to flatter him? The nobleman lifted an eyebrow. Maybe he understood.

I finished the poem, saying each line perfectly, without a lapse of memory. " 'Thus scops are fated to wander,' " I concluded. *My most confident performance so far!* " 'They meet generous people, eager to make a good name for themselves with heroic deeds and gift-giving—folk who appreciate a fine song, and who have as their reward glory, and a good reputation under heaven.' " It was over. I had done my best.

The listeners in Osgar's hall were beginning to talk again now, and as moments passed, my confidence began to ebb away. How had Osgar himself liked the tale? I couldn't bring myself to look up at him again to see his reaction. No one was calling out to me the way my traveling companions had, to tell me what they thought of my tale. I didn't know whether to sit down on the stool, return to my place by the wall, or step forward to the high table. So I stood alone in the middle of the hall until the steward appeared again at my elbow and said in a low voice, "Come this way."

He led me to the door of the hall, and stopped just outside to hand me my satchel, and to press into my hand a new silver penny. "My lord Osgar thanks you," he said as I blinked and strained to see him in the dusk. "It was a fine old lay you told tonight—one these nobles know well."

So Osgar probably *had* understood my flattery! "Will

Lord Osgar want me to come back, do you think?" I blurted out, clutching the penny so hard its edges dug into my palm.

"I don't think so, boy. When Osgar chooses a scop, it will be someone"—he searched for a phrase—"someone with skill honed by more years than yours. If you like, they'll find a place for you to sleep in the stable with your horse," he added. "You can move on in the morning after you've rested."

That was all. The steward disappeared back through the great doors.

I almost ran after him—I'd never wanted anything so much as the hall's warmth and light! Instead, I slumped hopelessly against the wall. *I was once a cherished daughter. I had a place of love and honor at my mother's hearth. . . .* After another minute I shuffled off to find the stables and Winter.

They'd snubbed Winter up to a rail along with several guests' horses. His coat showed the signs of a good brushing. Osgar would have made a scrupulous master, I thought forlornly as I crouched beside the rail.

Winter put his nose down and lipped at my shorn hair. I pushed his head away. "Your grass is on the ground, stupid," I said, my voice empty.

"We've come for our horses, boy."

I jerked in surprise at the sound of a voice just behind me, and almost dropped my book into the pile of grass. A group of men in ring mail and leather armor were entering the stable—the first guests to leave the hall, I guessed. I scrambled up, shoving my book back into the bag.

"That's not the stable lad. Isn't he the young scop from Osgar's hall?" said one of the other men. To me, all the faces in this group were shadowed, but the band's leader leaned a little closer to me, then shrugged.

"Mmm. Sorry. Hey, one of you," he called back over his shoulder to his companions as they proceeded down the row of horses, "find a stable hand and tell him we're taking our mounts, or they'll have us for horse thieves."

I should go, too, I decided, picking up Winter's blanket and throwing it over his back, then heaving the saddle up on top of it, almost missing my mark as Winter danced away. I knew it would be wiser to spend the night in this shelter, but I didn't want to stay where I had failed.

"That's *your* horse?" Once again the same voice took me by surprise, and I stumbled up against Winter's side in panic. Here was the leader of the band of guests coming back through the shadows, leading his own mount, which even in this dim light looked scrawny and ill fed. The man himself was tall, with a wild head of black hair and an unkempt beard. "Where'd you get a war stallion, boy?" he demanded.

"He was given to me," I answered, gripping Winter's girth strap with weak fingers. The man looked doubtful. My disappointment and loneliness flared up into desperate anger.

"You don't believe it?" I almost shouted at him. "You don't believe I could win such a prize with my skill?"

"I heard you tonight," the man replied evenly. "You're only beginning in your profession, and that horse is a rich gift."

A gift from Mother. I turned my attention quickly to loosening Winter's tether rope. I could not stop the tears this time, but I hoped no one would see them in the dark. Furtively I drew an arm across my cheeks, then clambered onto Winter's back with the help of the rail to which he'd been tied. I needed to end this conversation, and get away from all these unwelcome questions.

"Where're you going?" The man had mounted, too, and came trotting up behind me.

"This is my horse," I hissed through clenched teeth. "Ask the steward if you don't believe me."

"Hold there." I guessed that the tears were showing after all—I felt the hot trickles cooling on my face. "I'll take your word he's yours—although you do ride him like a half-filled sack of meal," the man added under his breath. "Where are you off to?" He rode alongside me now, and I slowed Winter's pace.

"That's my concern," I said, tired of his attentions. "I make my own way."

The man suddenly urged his horse directly across Winter's path, making both of us draw up abruptly. Furious, I opened my mouth to yell, but the man cut me off.

"Please hear me! You made mistakes tonight, boy, but don't be so stupid that you end up dead. You shouldn't be riding alone in the dark. Either stay here until morning, or come to our camp." He pointed in a direction I was still too angry to note. "I'm called Wil," he added after a second's pause. "You might need to tell the camp guards that, if you come."

After that he shouted for his men to follow him. I stayed where I was as they all rode past me.

"You with that lot?" It was the stable hand whom the group of men had hunted up. He had come walking along the line of horses, checking on those that were left behind as the band of twenty or so men left the stable yard.

"No." I went to turn Winter toward the market street. Maybe I could hunt down my band of farmers and rejoin them. Then I stopped. "Who's that man who spoke to me?"

"A thane from north of the Humber, I've heard, from Eoforwic, or thereabout. Lost his lands to Rægnald, is what he says. Brought his friends here looking for a lord to serve—maybe they're hoping to make themselves retainers of Osgar's household, I don't know. Their camp's just beyond the north gate."

I squinted out into the lowering darkness and saw the last horseman pass out of sight. I turned back to the stable hand, but he had gone. After another minute, I gave Winter a loose rein and sent him trotting after the others.

It wasn't the stable worker's words that made me follow

them, it was something that Wil had said. *"Please hear me!"*
These words and my dim impression of the man's dark-
bearded face came together in my head, joining another
memory of angry words uttered in the night.

I would ride out to that camp. I would find out if Wil was
the man I thought he was.

15

WIL OF EOFORWIC

WIL'S CAMP STOOD A FEW HUNDRED YARDS OUTSIDE THE WALLS surrounding Cirenceaster. His company had pitched their tents in a fallow field. I stopped Winter at the edge of camp. The men who had come from Osgar's hall were staking out their horses, lugging the saddles and bridles to four nearby wagons that had been arranged in a semicircle. In moments most of them had gone into their tents, and I let Winter jog over to the sentry.

"Wil told me to come," I said to the guard. The man looked me over, then nodded and helped me picket my big horse.

"Go to the largest of the tents in the middle of the camp. That's Wil's," he said.

My feet slowed as I approached the center tent. It was made of thick wool dyed a rusty red color, and the light from candles inside made it glow gently, like a great red flower on the black field. "If Wil is the man you think he is," I said to myself, "he has looked you over already, and clearly he does not see Ælfwyn of Mercia in the gloomy little scop from Osgar's hall." I needed a protector—my few days of traveling alone had taught me that. I scratched my fingers through my short hair, then walked forward with determination until I reached the carved wooden poles that held open the doorway of the tent.

The guard at the tent's entrance made way for me at the mention of Wil's name, just as the horse sentry had. I entered and took in the scene before me.

"I still don't understand why we've come here to this worthless town to be guests of a lesser nobleman. We sit drinking Osgar's thick ale, and listening to his colt of a scop—"

"Hold there, Kenelm." I thought I recognized Wil's low voice. Yes, there he was, speaking at the center of a small gathering of men. "You must be a fool, or at least very short of memory to call Cirenceaster worthless. Cirenceaster is a rich place. And if you don't see by now why friendship with Osgar will particularly help our cause . . ." Wil fell silent; he had spotted me by the door.

"The boy scop from Osgar's hall," he said, announcing my presence to the rest of the men in his little circle. Heads turned. I felt the group sizing me up. "I told him he could join us here," Wil explained. He motioned for me to come closer. I stepped forward, but gasped when I saw Kenelm. He was the young thane of Mercia who had met me in Lunden.

Kenelm—what was *he* doing here, I wondered in consternation. Kenelm, who had brought his father Cuthwine's message to me. This was a person who had met Ælfwyn, daughter of Æthelflæd, several times over, who had dined and conversed with her in daylight and at close quarters. My feet had stopped moving toward Wil. I wanted to run out of the tent and all the way back to Winter, who would carry me far away from Cirenceaster and this Mercian thane who could recognize me. My eyes locked helplessly on Kenelm's face and I saw that he had flushed with recognition . . .

. . . and with embarrassment. He looked quickly at Wil, then strode over to where I stood.

"I enjoyed your entertainment tonight, scop. My words a moment ago weren't kind—I'm sorry."

He knows me only as the scop!

"No, Kenelm." It was Wil again. "Don't lie to the scop about his poor performance. Come here, boy!" He waved me over impatiently now.

Even those who had seen Lady Æthelflæd's daughter clearly with their own eyes, it seemed, were not prepared to find her in such an unexpected place, looking like a filthy servant boy. Warily, I joined the ring of men.

"You're young to be riding alone," Wil said as I sat down beside Kenelm. "Did you lose your master? Wasn't there some older scop who taught you?"

"I—I lost my place in the home where I was born," I said, deciding to tell a little of the truth, and hoping they wouldn't ask more. "As a child I had teachers who helped me to read, and gave me poetry and stories. I thought I could use what I remembered of that to find a new place in some other lord's hall."

"So you've not learned from *any* scop," Wil said, shaking his head, "and you were surprised when Osgar didn't want you?" I hung my head. "Do you want to know why he sent you away?" Wil snapped. This question brought my head up with a jerk. I bit my lip, and after a moment I nodded.

"Wil, it's late for this kind of talk tonight," Kenelm interrupted mildly. "Perhaps we ought to offer the boy a bed first, and scold him later."

"Mmm," Wil said with a quick nod of his dark head, "probably you're right. We've had enough talk tonight." He did look tired, his eyes red, the skin sagging on his face like that of a man older than he was. The men began to get to their feet. "You can have a place in our camp, if you like, while we're at Cirenceaster," Wil offered gruffly.

"I thank you. I'd like to stay—for a little while," I responded.

"You haven't even asked him his name yet, have you, Wil?" said one of the thanes good-naturedly. "And you're giving him a bed in our camp, did I hear? Next thing you'll be calling the boy to our council circle."

"It's Widsith—Widsith's my name, I mean," I told Wil quickly, half-afraid he'd change his mind.

"Widsith"— he glowered at me—"a good name for a traveler. You've no family?"

"Lost," was what I said out loud. *Lost through death, and through betrayal.*

"Mine is lost, too," Wil said savagely. I stepped back, alarmed at the sadness and anger filling his voice. I bowed, trying not to let Wil shake me any further, and headed for the door to find some place outside to sleep.

"No, boy." Wil pointed to a pile of blankets. "Wrap yourself in one of those. You can sleep inside with us."

"Good night, Widsith." It was Kenelm passing on his way to his own bed, polite as ever. He still showed no sign of recognizing me.

"Good night," I replied, comforted, and went to find a corner where I could sleep.

I was one of the first in the tent to wake the next morning. I'd never been an early riser, but since I'd left my uncle's court I'd had only cold, hard beds, as well as the racing heart of a fugitive.

I crept outside and went to check on Winter. Wil found me there just as the rising sun touched the field.

"Your horse faring well?" he asked.

"I think so," I answered timidly. Winter was tearing at the grass and showing me the white of his eye, warning me not to lead him away from his breakfast unless I wanted trouble.

"Fine animal," Wil said with a yawn. "He's got an ugly color to him, though—what would you call it, brown dapple?

But that's a good short back, clean legs. Has the horse got a name?"

"Winter," I replied, then added hastily when I saw his quizzical look, "they told me he was born in wintertime."

"You're a strange lad," Wil said in a quiet voice. "What made you try to be a scop, without any training?"

"I told you, I've read things, learned some stories and poetry. . . ."

"But knowing a tale and telling one are two different things," Wil broke in impatiently. "Hi, you!" he called out to the sentry posted with the horses, who had been at Osgar's hall the night before. "The story this scop told last night," Wil demanded, "have you heard it before?"

"Aye," the man replied, coming closer, "I remembered hearing some of it before."

"So what was wrong with the way the boy did it?" Wil wanted to know.

"Well," the man considered, "he said the words all right. I thought there might be something Osgar didn't like. It was when the scop said something slow, and the lord kind of wrinkled his forehead, as if he wasn't happy with what he heard. It was just a line about two men who—what was it, now?—who won a battle over their enemies, I think. 'Hewed them down at Heorot' was the way the scop said it." He turned to me. "It wasn't a bad show, boy, for such a young one as you."

"Why did you choose to make that line so clear for Osgar's ears, Widsith?" Wil pressed.

"Because of the hall," I admitted. "I saw the hart horns Osgar had hung up, and I thought maybe he knew Heorot from the poem. I don't know why I thought he would. It was stupid."

"Yes, stupid," Wil replied quickly. "Osgar did understand the line, and you didn't."

I didn't know what to say. I just stared at Wil. He began to quote the lines from my performance:

> Hrothwulf and Hrothgar kept peace together
> After they gained victory over the invading horde
> Hewed them down at Heorot.

"You say you mentioned Heorot, the golden hall, to win Osgar's favor by comparing it to his own feasting place," Wil repeated, "but you don't know who Hrothwulf and Hrothgar were, do you?"

I shook my head, abashed.

"Hrothgar was a Danish king," Wil explained, his dark eyes fixed on me, "and Hrothwulf his brother's son. Together they beat back the invaders at Heorot, it is true, but there is more to their story. Heorot burned in that battle, and later Hrothwulf took the throne from Hrothgar's two young sons, killing one of them. So, boy, you may have meant to flatter your host, but instead you compared his hall to a site of ruin and treason."

"I haven't read about that anywhere!" I protested.

"Those stories aren't written, boy. They're told, and sung," Wil retorted. "Did you never hear a passable scop perform the story in the household where you were raised?" he asked querulously.

I shook my head. "I—I didn't listen to them very well, I guess."

Wil snorted. "All my life I've rubbed shoulders with Danes in the north country, and sometimes fought with them and with Norsemen, none of whom could read a word—men who would scrape the gold from a decorated page and use the parchment to clean a cooking pot. Still, those men could tell a tale.

"The last night I spent in one of the Norse camps, I was bound and bashed on the head so I could hardly stand." His voice was quiet now, and the guard leaned in, listening as intently as I. "I could hear one Norseman boasting about his skill in battle that day. He said he'd fought against one opponent until both their swords broke, and they struggled hand to hand until a stone, a gift from the gods, appeared beneath his fingers in the mud. He picked it up and with the rock in his hand felled the other man with a single blow that cracked his helmet." One of Wil's hands came up unconsciously to rub his temple. "My head ached like a rotten tooth as I lay on my side where they'd thrown me in the mud. But there I lay, listening to the man talk, so taken with his story that only as he finished did I realize that I was the very opponent the Norseman spoke of. He'd improved the tale so I hardly recognized myself."

The guard burst out laughing at this. Wil waited until he quieted to add, "That night after I worked free of my bonds, I let that man sleep on safely with his companions, and I left the camp. Anyone who could make a story like that out of our clumsy fight deserved at least one more night in this life."

"You probably didn't want to bring the whole Norse camp down on you just so you could pay him back that blow with the rock," said the guard, standing up to return to his post, and laughing again at his leader's reluctant grin. Then Wil left, too, but not before he'd told me where I could get some breakfast.

A strange, argumentative man, I thought as I sat a few moments longer watching Winter crop grass. That long black hair, the wild beard—I still couldn't tell if he'd invited me here out of pity, or just because he couldn't bear to let my poor performance stand without correction.

I stood up. It was really no surprise that Wil of Eoforwic made me feel this way. He and I had vexed each other from the first night we'd met, almost exactly a year ago in the fields outside Lunden, when he'd still been Wilfrid, the Northumbrian king, and I was Ælfwyn of Mercia.

16

A JOURNEY CHARM

AFTER MORE THAN A WEEK IN THEIR COMPANY, I WAS NO closer to knowing what Wil and his twenty-odd companions were doing in Cirenceaster. I had food enough, and I felt safe for the first time since I'd become a small and vulnerable person alone in the world. But I was not invited to any more meetings in the red tent, and so I kept wondering.

Each morning an assortment of strangers rode into camp and entered the red tent to meet with Wil. All of these were English thanes, as far as I could tell, but I could not guess who the visitors might be, nor what they might want with a man who had once been King of Eoforwic. Still, I kept my eyes and ears open, hoping to learn something.

And Wil kept his eye on me. No later than the time of the midday meal, he would emerge and shout my name. He needed to look over the horses, he'd tell me, or search out a pair of boots sent to be mended and not returned yet. Sometimes he'd just announce that he needed to clear his head. "Walk with me, boy," he would order, and I'd half trot along beside him as he strode off on whatever errand he'd named.

I found Wil's conversation an irksome mixture of barbs and useful information. My poor horsemanship was a favorite theme. Wil often mentioned that I needed to sit farther forward when the horse lifted from a trot into a canter. What Wil should have said was "stop being terrified of falling off," or maybe even "give your warhorse to someone who can really ride."

There were other things Wil wanted to talk about—things I hoped I might actually be able to learn. Almost always our conversations touched upon the skills of a good scop. Sometimes Wil would talk about other singers he'd heard—English and Danish scops who'd told tales during his days in Eoforwic. I always sat and absorbed these lessons with an ear pricked to hear how much he would say about his former life, or possibly his future plans. I was always disappointed.

I tried to make myself useful around camp in those first days, although no one had asked me to do anything in particular. One afternoon I screwed up my courage and went out to the field where the horses were kept. I asked the guard, whose name was Swithulf, if he needed my help.

"That one needs a fresh picket," Swithulf grunted, nodding toward an underfed black mare—not much more than a pony, really—who had cropped every inch of grass in the circle around her picket stake. She's a lot smaller than Winter, I reassured myself, gulping. All I had to do was grab her picket line, pull up the stake, and walk calmly a few yards farther out into the pasture where I could tamp the stake down again.

When I touched her rope, the mare jerked her head up and stood stock-still. She made no other movement as I worked the stake loose, and I breathed a sigh of relief as I gathered in the slack and gave her a little tug forward.

"Come on, girl," I said, keeping my voice low and steady. She took a step toward me, then another.

And then suddenly she was snaking her head sideways to nip at the nearest horse, squealing as she danced in a half-circle, and I saw that she was getting ready to aim a kick in my direction. With a yelp of my own I stamped the picket stake down into the turf right where I was standing and dashed out of her reach. Behind me I heard Swithulf laughing.

"I've waited to move her all day," he admitted. "Meanest one of the bunch. C'mon. We'll do it together." We did, although it was clear to me that Swithulf could have done the job himself, since all I did was pull up my weakly fixed stake and put it in the ground again where he told me to. He watched the mare and kept one hand casually on the rope with just enough tautness to keep her under control. Afterward he let me try lugging buckets from the nearby stream to water the horses, but after the third one was overturned by an anxious nose or a nervous hoof, he told me not to bother.

"We'll just lead them down to the stream to drink," Swithulf said. He caught me by the wrist as I stepped back toward the herd. "No, boy, not now. We take them in threes, and you couldn't..." He broke off, and then finished politely, "You just water your own horse. That's all the help I need."

They never let me do much more in the pasture after that. I did some fetching and carrying for the camp cooks, lugged firewood a few times each week, but found little else to do except eat, sleep, sit in the shade, practice my riding, and wait for Wil to call me.

On the evening of my seventh day in camp, Wil and his men headed to Osgar's hall again for another meal. I stayed behind, saying I was too tired to go, but in truth not wanting to show my face in the hall after my lackluster performance. Alone except for the three guards Wil had left behind, I huddled down in the shadow of one of the smaller tents and gnawed on the handful of sour plums they'd given me to eat.

I felt restless. At least with the farmers, we had been progressing along the road every day. Remaining in Wil's camp had seemed all right a few days back when hunger and homelessness had seemed unbearable. But now I began worrying again that the king's men were surely still searching for his missing niece.

Maybe I should leave, I thought to myself, spitting a plum stone into a clump of grass. Keep moving. I bit into the next fruit and felt my mouth twist into a painful pucker—it was the sourest plum of the lot. A richer patron might feed me better, at least. . . .

". . . isn't what I planned for this week, but if the thanes from eastern Mercia need to see us, I think we have to make the journey." It was Wil's voice, and the sound was coming closer. I crouched down, keeping absolutely still.

"How many men will you take with you?" It sounded like the voice of a ginger-haired thane named Eadwine who often acted as one of Wil's close advisers. "It would not help our cause if Osgar saw most of us ride off immediately after suggesting we pledge our loyalty to him."

"That's right." The footfalls stopped. I guessed that Wil and Eadwine stood just on the opposite side of the tent where I was lurking. Anyone would take me for a meddler, a spy, should they find me listening. I squeezed my eyes shut, wishing I could disappear but wanting to know more. "I'll take only the boy from Osgar's hall. And we'll be back in under a week—perhaps we can make the journey in five days, with my horse rested and better fed than it used to be."

"The fledgling scop?" Eadwine sounded incredulous. "I didn't think you'd decided to trust the lad yet. He's not even allowed in our council—"

"I have a plan for the boy, Eadwine. I could use the trip to learn more about him, to make sure he has or learns the skills necessary."

Wil wanted to take *me* along? So there *was* a reason why he had invited me to stay. The footsteps had begun again, and the voices were moving away from me. A short journey, I thought, alone with Wil. . . .

"Widsith!" Wil was calling me, and from far enough away, I judged, that he would not guess that I'd been almost close enough to touch him a few minutes earlier. "Widsith!" I scrambled up and took off toward the sound at a run, reminding myself to look surprised when Wil made his proposal.

We left the next morning, going east. It was to be a fast ride, I'd been told, but not until we'd covered the first day's ground did I understand that we would spend almost every daylight hour in the saddle. It was a steady and grinding pace for mount and rider alike, much faster than the leisurely rate my party of churls had set for themselves when I'd traveled with them a few weeks earlier, but one that the horses could keep up almost indefinitely with enough food, water, and overnight rest.

That evening I slid down from the saddle, exhausted. Winter seemed well enough after the long day's ride, and when he was grazing contentedly, I hobbled over to the level spot where Wil was making camp. He seemed quite fresh, I thought. Obviously *his* body understood how to ride at a trot without jarring the bones with every jounce.

"Got your supper with you, scop?" Wil asked, chewing at a strip of dried meat he held.

"My supper? I . . ." He had expected me to bring my own food? "I . . . I didn't—" *Stupid! What made you think he'd*

just keep feeding you? In five days' journey you'll begin to
starve! You'll have to look for a settlement, buy something
with one of your coins. Wil was laughing at me, I finally noticed. With a sheepish grin, I caught the strip of meat and
hunk of flat bread he tossed my way, and I sat down to eat.

After we'd finished our meal, I crawled to my pile of gear
and slumped against it in the dusk. My eyes were closing.

"Widsith! It's time to pay me for that fine meal I just fed
you!" Wil said loudly. I jerked upright. "I want a song
tonight, and I've paid for it with a day's ration. You'll give me
a song before we bed down."

A song. Yes, I nodded, I'd sing for him. Stiffly I moved a
little closer to where he sat in the darkness. Didn't I know a
charm? Yes, something I'd recited once to one of my tutors
in Lunden. I thought it through, trying to match the words
with a tune I used to hear in the marketplace when I'd go
with Gytha—music a beggar used to play on a wooden pipe
of some sort. I began, singing softly:

With this rod I protect myself,
Against the wounding blade or blow, against all fear
    upon the land.
A charm of vanquishing I chant; a rod of vanquish-
    ing I carry.
Winning by word, winning by deed,
No nightmare possess me, nor belly distress me,
Nor fear for my life arise.

It was hard to remember the middle part of the charm, which was filled with the names of apostles and prophets meant to ward off evil on a journey. I hummed the tune through again as I searched my memory quickly for an ending. There had been something about leading and protecting, and Matthew for a helmet, Mark for a shield, and then the conclusion: *let me meet with friends* . . . something like that. No, first *forth I go—*

> *Forth I go: let me meet with friends.*
> *I call upon God to give me good journey,*
> *And gentle winds along the shore.*
> *I have heard how the winds have rolled back the*
> *   waves,*

Hmm, a charm for sea travel wasn't exactly what we needed; maybe Wil would just remember the other parts.

> *Steadily saved men from all their enemies.*
> *Let me meet with friends, stay free of foes,*
> *In the holy hand of the Lord of Heaven,*
> *As long as I dwell in life.*

"Amen." I sang the last word, ending on an uncertain note at odds with the charm's bid for sureness and safety. I hung my head. Wil wouldn't like what I'd sung—somehow I felt sure of that.

"Better, scop," Wil announced, surprisingly. "You chose better this time. That charm is a fine offering for a pair of travelers on their first night together. But who taught you to use your voice outside?" He snorted. "I'm sitting not five paces from you, and at times I could hardly hear the tune. Do it again, boy, with some power. Sing from your chest!"

So I began again, singing lustily this time, but after just a few lines Wil stopped me.

"I didn't say bellow, did I? There's a difference between shouting and singing. A scop shouldn't have to shout, unless he's in a room of drunken oafs."

"That happens often enough," I muttered.

"Try once again," Wil said, ignoring me. "Sing out strongly, but don't yell." I had to do it three more times while Wil sat, listening intently, fiddling with something in his hands. "Enough for tonight," he said at last. "Go get some sleep. I'll check the horses."

He stood up and stalked past me, and that was all. No further praise or criticism, no warning about when I might expect another such exercise. I stood up and stumbled back to my blankets. By now I should have learned to expect Wil's abruptness, I thought sleepily as I lay down, just as I had become accustomed to uneven ground for my bed. I squirmed onto my side, trying to find a comfortable position for my shoulder and hip.

"It was a good song."

With a gasp, I rolled over and looked up. Wil's returning footfalls had been so silent I hadn't heard him come near. His voice was right above my head.

"A journey charm," he said, his voice warmer than it had been all day. " 'With this rod I protect myself.' " He bent down and placed something next to my hand. My fingers explored it—a wooden cross, made of two sticks bound at the juncture with a length of leather thong. " 'A rod of vanquishing I carry.' " With a grin he reached down and unsheathed my knife, which I'd placed on the ground just beneath the edge of my saddle. Holding it up gingerly by the point, he showed me the cross formed by hilt and blade. "And we've got my sword, too." He jerked his head toward his own gear, atop which rested the weapon. "Think that's enough protection to get us safely there and back?" I nodded feebly. "Good night, Widsith." Wil's soft laughter was the last thing I heard before I buried my head in my arms and slept.

I awoke to rain and the faint beginning of grey light in the dark sky. Wil hurried us into the saddle before our blankets could get very wet, but little good it did us, I thought as we rode through the increasing drizzle. My cloak was damp and beginning to cling to me. The blankets tied behind me on my saddle wouldn't fare any better. Everything we owned would be soaked well before the sky lightened enough to show the clouds massing above us.

By the time it was light enough for me to see Wil riding ahead of me, I was shivering. I wished we were walking instead of riding—I'd have kept warmer that way. At our brief midday stop Wil made me run in a ring around him while he held the horses.

"Never seen any but skinny women so prone to cold," I heard him muttering as I trotted in my circle. The exercise helped make my blood flow faster again, but unfortunately it didn't last. A few hours into our afternoon ride I was shaking so hard I could barely keep my seat. Wil looked doubtfully at me, and then peered into the distance.

"We need to reach our meeting place tonight," he said. "Can you ride a little farther?" I tried to nod, but the movement almost overbalanced me, and I grabbed at the saddle and Winter's mane with clumsy fingers to keep from tumbling off. With a curse, Wil swung down from his horse and came to Winter's side. He knotted his horse's reins around the ropes holding my gear. "Move forward, boy," he commanded, and I tried to do as he'd said, inching up so I was nearly off the saddle straddling Winter's neck. Wil took a hank of Winter's mane in his hand and lightly vaulted into the saddle behind me. "Good thing you're still small," he said, reaching around me to grab Winter's reins, "and your horse is big. He's strong enough to carry both of us for a while."

I'd been struggling against the cold too long to protest. One of Wil's arms encircled my waist, and the other crooked around me to guide the horse. I tried to sit stiffly at first, but I was exhausted, and before long I was leaning back against

Wil's broad chest, swaying along with him to the cadence of Winter's steps, and relying on Wil's arms to keep me from falling. Warm and safe—I gave in to the strangeness of touching him, and somehow it was no longer very strange.

I vaguely remember reaching a hut, and an old man and woman scuttling out into the rain when Wil offered them a coin. We stumbled into their smoky hovel and Wil lowered me onto the pile of straw that served for a bed. Sleep was all I wanted, although at some point he tried to make me eat. I was aware that Wil went out, came back, and went out again, seeing to the horses, gathering damp wood that hissed and steamed when he fed it gingerly, stick by stick, to the flames on the hearth. I remember Wil lying down on the straw, his back to me, feet to the fire.

He had held me, as if it were no more peculiar to touch and help a companion than to gentle a horse, build a fire, make food. And I had felt safe, as well as something else. . . . I wanted to feel that again. After a moment I squirmed closer until my back pressed against his.

"You're a leech, Widsith," he mumbled, but he didn't move away, and in a few moments we both slept.

In the morning the sun was shining, the fire was out, and I was very much ashamed. "You lost at least half a day's journey because of me," I said, hanging my head as we rode out. Today Wil rode beside me on his own horse.

"You owe me a night's performance," he said, squinting into the rising sun, "and I'll want another one this evening, after I've met with the people I've come to see. So I guess you'll have to start now. Here's what I want you to learn." He recited a wisdom poem to me, a maxim, and then made me tell the words back to him as we rode along, expecting me to bring my own emotion and inflection to the lines.

"Winter is the coldest time, spring chillest (it is cold longest)," I recited slowly, frowning over the next lines: "Summer has the most sun, the sun is hottest." Was Wil poking fun at my sorry reaction to yesterday's cold and rain? I glanced sideways at him. His expression was thoughtful.

"Do that last line again, boy," he said solemnly. "I'm not sure I heard you."

"Summer has the most sun," I repeated sullenly, "the sun is hottest . . ." Wil *was* making fun.

"Say you were the scop of some nobleman, singing in his hall each night," Wil called out, lifting his horse into a trot, which I had to follow, "and say you'd made a fool of yourself in the cold one winter day—out hunting with the lord's party, and had to be carried home stiff and shivering, something like that. What would you do if someone asked you to tell that maxim in the hall afterward?"

"Tell it, I guess," I called back, thumping uncomfortably in my saddle and wishing we could go a little slower, "if I had to."

"And what if no one asked to hear that maxim?" was Wil's next question.

"Huh?" What if no one asked? "I'd—I'd count myself

lucky, and sing about some battle instead," I answered, confused.

"No!" Wil roared, wheeling his horse around and halting so abruptly that I almost ran them down before I could bring Winter to a stand. "No! You would choose the maxim yourself, and tell it to them *hoping* for their laughter. Don't you see, boy? A laugh at your expense, that's a handful of treasure for a performer! You can't throw that away out of pride, unless you're a bigger fool than . . ."

A crackling rustle made Wil shut his mouth midsentence.

"Stay back," he told me in a low voice. "There's something in the woods."

Suddenly a terrible din rose all around us. Winter half reared, dumping me onto the soft ground beneath him. Men had appeared, rising up out of the countryside. They surrounded us, yelling and beating on their wooden shields with drawn swords and knives and fists.

I crawled clear of Winter's stamping feet, and tried to catch his reins, but other hands grabbed them before I could. I heard shouting in English, so these weren't foreign raiders. Still, they looked far from friendly. I got to my feet, wishing I had the nerve to use the knife hidden beneath my leather vest.

Wil was still on his horse, but a man on either side held the bridle, and two more men gripped each of his legs and arms, all of them together keeping the horse immobile and Wil trapped in the saddle. I tried to count the men who had surprised us, and lost count somewhere above fifteen. There might have been more than twenty of them—I couldn't be sure. One of them was coming forward to stand in front of Wil.

"What are you doing on this road?" he demanded curtly.

"The way is open to any traveler," Wil growled in answer. "We have nothing of value. Let us go."

The spokesman eyed Wil sardonically, and gestured toward me and Winter. "You'd make a couple of sturdy slaves for the Northumbrian markets, and you've got at least one fine horse—there's profit here for one who wishes to take it. But I'm asking for something less costly from you. I want to know what your purpose is on this road."

"If your trade is thieving, as your words suggest, I can't think of any reason to tell you more about myself," retorted Wil, setting his mouth in a grim line. The other man looked annoyed, and whispered for a moment with another man beside him.

"We are waiting for someone who calls himself Wil of Eoforwic. We expected him before sundown yesterday evening. Did you pass his party as you traveled?" was the man's next question. Wil's face lightened in an instant.

"I am Wil of Eoforwic," he answered, then looked around in bafflement and then anger as the crowd around us burst into laughter.

"Wil of Eoforwic is a lord who leads a group of fighters," the spokesman said, shaking his head. "Don't worry, we don't want to rob you, but don't lie to us! The man we're waiting for isn't coming alone." Wil's frustration was about to flow out in a stream of angry words. In a panic, I opened my mouth.

"He *is* Wil of Eoforwic," I said. Even to myself I sounded petulant, no more worthy of their attention than a child arguing with his elders. The spokesman turned around and stared at me. I swallowed. What would convince them that Wil was who he claimed to be? I cleared my throat.

"Against the Norse, at Eoforwic," I said, trying to speak out boldly, the way Wil had been teaching me, "this man beat against his opponent's shield until both of their swords broke. Then they struggled hand to hand until a stone, a gift from the devil himself, appeared beneath the Norse foe's fingers in the mud, and he picked it up and felled Wil of Eoforwic with a blow that cracked his helmet. Seeing he was outnumbered, my master lay still where they'd thrown him in the mud until nightfall, when he worked free of his bonds, single-handedly killed all his foes as they slept, and rode on to Cirenceaster, where bold men continue to flock to his camp." I paused for breath, then added, "So say all his followers: Eadwine of Gleawceaster, Kenelm of Lincylene—"

"Young Kenelm?" The spokesman's face split into a grin. "I jounced that boy on my knee before he ever rode a horse. Know his father, too." He looked at Wil again, then looked back at me. After a moment, he made a little bow.

"Wil of Eoforwic," he said, "you and your companion are

welcome. Our camp lies over that rise." He pointed a little farther down the road. "We can talk there."

Now I looked at Wil, and he met my eye with a little smile. He nodded his thanks, and then, hesitantly, crooked a finger at me, beckoning me to come. Did he mean that I could join him? Maybe he was beginning to trust me! Or was he only concerned for my safety. . . .

I thought of what Wil had been trying to teach me these past two days. He'd explained that I must restrain my own passions, and think what the listeners would value most. At this moment Wil seemed to be offering me a place within his circle of trusted friends, but he had trained me too thoroughly over these last days. I suspected it wasn't yet the right time to follow my own desires and accept such a gift.

"I'll stay here with the horses," I told my master, and after a moment, he nodded again.

"Help him tie them to a tree," was all he said to the others before he turned to walk back down the road with the man who had challenged him.

It was late afternoon when Wil returned, walking alone. We rode back westward, the declining sun casting long shadows all around us. Wil said nothing about his talks beyond the hill. I hadn't honestly expected him to, but still, the lowering silence between us was strange. We ate quietly, settled the horses, and bedded down near each other.

I was remembering yesterday, when I'd been so cold. The feeling of his arms around me when he'd had to guide my horse. Last night I'd moved to sleep with my back against his. I shivered, remembering it, wondering how I'd been so brave, wishing I were brave enough to do it again.

Out of the darkness Wil's large hand came to rest over my small cold one.

"Sing the journey charm, Widsith. We may want it again for the return."

Leaving my hand beneath his, I turned onto my side. In the dark, I knew, Wil would not see the smile of relief I wore. Nor, if I worked to keep my voice steady, would he guess at the sudden roughness in my throat.

"With this rod I protect myself," I whispered to Wil, fingering the little sticks bound into a cross, which I'd tucked under my belt next to Mother's dagger, "against the wounding blade or blow, against all fear upon the land."

17

A Fine Song

My first duty, when we got back to our camp at Cirenceaster, was to tell the tale of our journey to Wil's followers after our evening meal. I began with a description of the punishing storm, making them laugh at my helplessness in the face of cold, just as Wil had suggested. Then I sprang the rebel ambush upon my listeners, hoping to give them the same sort of shock we'd had on the road.

They loved it. I had to back away from the campfire, shaking my head and pointing to Wil as they began to ask me questions. Their leader would have to tell them what happened after that.

The next night, to my surprise, they asked me to perform again.

"What use is it to us to have a scop in the camp if he never gives us a song!" a burly thane shouted, and I was made to stand up, pushed out into the open space, and teased good-naturedly until I agreed to sing for them. I used the tune I'd remembered during my journey with Wil, but instead of a charm, I sang them a riddle and waited for them to guess the solution when I finished my song.

"Dough!" one man called out. "It's something that a woman makes, that grows, you said. Dough is the answer."

"How about a woman's belly, getting big with a child?" another member of Wil's camp shouted, and everyone laughed when I shrugged.

"That couldn't be right! Widsith doesn't know anything about women!" they joked, and I hid my face behind one hand, which made them laugh all the more. Both answers were correct—the riddle had a double meaning. But it was my own double nature that made my head spin that night. This performance—being Widsith—never ended. At least when I had been with Wil on the journey with just the two of us together I could sit shivering on a horse with his arms encircling me, or lie still, touching him, and just for a moment be the girl Ælfwyn, comforted, close to Wil.

"Give us another one, scop!"

I looked up at them, the men's faces laughing, expectant in the firelight. I made myself grin a boy's cocky smile back at them, and started to sing again.

Wil came looking for me later that evening.

"Osgar is feasting again tomorrow night, and he's asked us to come. I want you to be with our company in the hall, Widsith."

"Me? I—I'm not sure I should." Only two seven days'

time had passed since I had sung before Osgar and his guests. "They'll remember me, and they'll wonder why I'm back."

"That's none of their concern," Wil responded. "Osgar has said he'd welcome all who come with me. Besides, he's not likely to remember you, anyhow." I must have looked downcast, because Wil gave me a thump on my shoulder that nearly made me fall over my own feet. "Cheer up, little scop," he said curtly. "We'll make Osgar notice you before we're finished in Cirenceaster. So be ready tonight. Have your horse saddled by the time they ring for vespers inside the *tun*." With that, he was off.

We'll make Osgar notice you . . . What had Wil meant by that? I thought about it all day, and by the time I sat on Winter's back with the band that had gathered to go into the *tun*, I was still turning the question over in my mind. I sighed. Whatever his reasons, I wouldn't say no to Wil. The riders began to move out, and with a flap of my arms and legs, I urged Winter along beside them.

Wil was right. The steward spotted me as our party passed into the hall—I saw his eyes flick across my face and clothing when I walked by. But he said nothing, and as far as I could tell, Osgar remained ignorant that a certain mediocre young scop had returned for another meal.

I ate well that night, better than my first night in Osgar's hall, for now I was elbow to elbow with invited guests, and the servants made sure there was always food in front of us. I speared what meat I could reach onto the end of my mother's little dagger, ate the good wheat bread eagerly after days of modest barley-flour cakes in Wil's camp, and tried not to let the others see that I drank only a little ale.

In spite of my care, I must have drunk more than I could hold. Kenelm sat on one side of me, and I found myself smiling at his laughter even though I could not hear the jokes that prompted it. A little farther down the table I could make out Wil. He was speaking intently with the man on his left, a man whom I did not recognize as anyone from Wil's usual group of followers.

Wil saw me watching him, and tipped his head toward the steward. He was leading a tall, plainly dressed man who walked toward the very stool they had offered to me on my first night here.

The scop bowed to Osgar and the other nobles, then turned and bowed formally to the rest of us. I wrapped my arms around myself, suddenly feeling alone and a little cold, even though it was a warm night and I sat in a bright and crowded room.

The man took out a little bundle wrapped in oiled cloth and as he opened it, a murmur of appreciation rose from the nobles at the high table and spread around the crowd. He had brought a harp. From where I sat it appeared to be a ring of seasoned wood, darkened by many evenings spent in the smoke of great halls. It was much older than the harps I used to practice playing in Lunden, and much more beautiful. A delicate tracery of bright inlaid metal (perhaps it was even gold) glittered on either side of the strings, which were wound on wooden pegs above and below the central opening. The outer rim of the harp was about as wide across as the length of the scop's forearm, but it must not have been especially heavy, for he picked it up with one hand and braced it in the crook of his arm. With the other hand he touched the strings, and at the same time, he began to sing.

At first the plaintive tone of the scop's song was all I could understand. The words he sang—of danger, of isolation—didn't seem to make a story. They only stirred up a sense of dread inside me.

But then some of his words began to make pictures in my head. I saw a person alone, beset by enemies, yearning for a distant lover. And suddenly, I knew the song:

> *Wulf, my Wulf! My longing for you*
> *Has made me sick—your absence,*
> *My mournful mind—*

These were verses I had read in the months after I'd lost Mother, verses that seemed to echo the grief I carried with me everywhere during those days. The scop sang of rain. *Rain on the day they took her body away, rain and tears.* I hung my head as tears streamed down my face. By then the scop was finishing: " 'A person easily severs what's not united: our song together.' "

The verse lingered in the hall, along with the last note of the harpstrings. Then there was silence, except for the snarling of two dogs fighting over a pork knuckle beneath one of the tables. Someone growled out a warning to the dogs, and the bone was kicked away. By now the crowd was talking again. Furtively, I wiped my cheeks—no one must see these tears, least of all Wil.

Osgar was pleased with the night's performance. He called the scop over and gave him something. I saw a bright gleam, something silver and heavy. It was a rich armband, perhaps, or even a necklace—much more than Osgar had offered me. I leaned my head into my hands.

"He's done this more times than you, but that was no better than the riddles you gave us last night, Widsith." A hand pounded my back and I had to grip the table to keep my balance. It was Kenelm speaking more loudly than he ought. The ale had gone to his head just as it had to mine.

"Our host liked it well enough," I responded quietly. I missed Mother, I regretted my failure, and I was also starting to feel quite sick. Maybe the cooler air outside the hall would calm my stomach. I swung my legs over the bench and stood up, but before I took a step toward the door someone touched my shoulder.

"Slowly now, Widsith. A guest shouldn't go storming out." Wil had come up behind me and now he drew me back down to sit beside him on the bench I had just left.

"It's the drink. I need some air. Please." I pulled away from him. "I need to go."

Wil caught me again gently, as easily as he might confine

an unruly puppy. "Can you slip out softly, boy, and wait for us outside while I give our thanks to Osgar and apologize for not staying to hear the scop's second song?"

"You're leaving now, too?"

"I've heard news tonight that I need to discuss privately, and as soon as possible." Wil looked over his shoulder at Osgar. "Our host likes the new singer. He won't mind that we have to go early."

"That's a scop like a hundred others!" Kenelm leaned in toward us, nearly shouting. "We've heard you trying to teach our Widsith how best to tell a story, but see, all he needs is a harp, and Osgar will take him for a hearth-companion."

Wil frowned. "Go on now," he told me, "but wait for us outside, mind." He looked at Kenelm, who was holding up his drinking bowl, calling out to a servant carrying a skin of ale. "Take him with you," he added, and stumped off toward the high table.

The next day I sat in a corner of Wil's camp beside the pots and clay vessels they used to prepare food. I still didn't know what news had sent Wil galloping back to the red tent where he had shut himself up for the rest of the night with his closest advisers, and of course no one told me. After seeing last night's scop, I felt like a failure. The scop had a rare gift. My mother had once spoken to me of the great poet Cædmon's gift. I shut my eyes.

"Your teacher will give you Cædmon's poetry when you're ready, Wyn, but I want to tell you Cædmon's own story. Cædmon was only a poor cowherd, and he had never learned reading or writing, as you are learning now, little one." She stroked my cheek. "He couldn't even sing with his friends when they gathered to entertain themselves with stories and song."

"Was he afraid?" I wanted to know.

"Maybe he was. He hadn't yet discovered his gift."

"What do you mean, his gift?"

Mother drew me close—I remember the smell of her clean linen sleeve close to my face, a soft braid of her hair unbound for night, brushing against my neck. "One night Cædmon crept away from his friends, ashamed that he could not sing. He went to sleep with the animals, who would not care about his lack of skill. And that night in the barn, he dreamed of a man who spoke up and said, 'Cædmon, sing me something.' "

"But Cædmon couldn't, didn't you say?" I breathed.

"Yes," Mother answered, "that's what he believed, and he told the dream man so, but the man only replied, 'Nevertheless, you can.' "

"And then what happened?"

Mother shrugged. "Cædmon saw that he had to try, so he opened his mouth and out came beautiful verses."

"He couldn't do it before, and then suddenly he could?" I must have sounded doubtful.

"It was his gift," Mother told me. *"He found it when he tried."*

I couldn't remember what she'd said after that.

"The fever took her, girl"—Dunstan's broken voice.

I leaned my head against a tall clay jar, hugging my knees to my chest.

One easily severs what was never united . . . I wanted to whimper, to wail . . . *our song together.*

"Can you play?"

"Uh?" I scrambled to my feet, brushed away my tears. *Mother. Cædmon. That scop from last night and his cursed song!* Wil was standing in front of me. He was holding a harp—a smaller instrument than the one Osgar's scop had used, and made of bright new maple.

"Are you well, boy?"

I nodded. "Just the ale from last night," I mumbled, rubbing my head.

"I've had three of my men looking for you since the midday bell," he said crossly, "and you've been here all the time?" I nodded. Wil threw up his hand. "Well, can you play? That's what I'm asking."

Warily, I nodded again.

"Good. When you go into Osgar's hall again, you'll play this, and I'm sure you'll please him as much as the man we heard last night."

"But—but why?" was all I could think to say in my confusion. Wil planted his hands on his hips.

"If you succeed, we can talk about why. When can you be ready? A week?"

I only stared at him.

"Widsith, can you not hear me? How long will it take you to prepare? A week?" I looked away from him, trying to think. *Cædmon found his gift when he tried. That's what Mother told me.*

"A week, Widsith?"

"Two," I finally agreed, with a heavy heart.

I had to find a story, and although I ransacked the stolen book of poetry, nothing seemed right. In desperation, I lay on my back in the browning, end-of-summer grass, and searched my memory for something—the right thing—for this task Wil had assigned.

There was one possibility: a story I'd read over and over, translated from Latin to English and back again, and discussed with Gytha ad nauseam. On my own, there in the tall grass not far from where the horses grazed, I tried out its familiar words. I repeated them until each one came to my tongue almost before I thought about it. As I recited, I considered the things Wil had been saying to me about how a scop ought to perform. I remembered how, in the dusk with my company of farmers, I had let myself sing and speak easily. Maybe these words would draw a noble audience along in that same way.

◆ ◆ ◆

A few nights before our next meal in Osgar's hall, Wil called me to him and asked me to recite what I had prepared. I stood in front of him, hands at my sides, trying not to show my nerves.

"This present life," I began shakily, "is such a thing as when you sit a-feasting with aldormen and thanes in wintertime, the fire burning in the hall, the rains and storms and snows outside. Then in comes a little sparrow, and flies swiftly through the hall. He comes in through one door, and departs through another on the other side. During the time he's inside, he's not touched by the winter's storm. But that's just the blink of an eye, the smallest space of time, and then the bird is out in the storm again. That's as much of life as anyone can see—what a sparrow sees when he's in the hall, briefly out of the storm, but just about to fly back into it."

That was all—every word of the story I'd been preparing for nearly a fortnight. Anxiously I waited, standing there. How would Wil react? Probably the words I'd picked wouldn't be to his taste, I suddenly realized. And it wasn't even a real poem, just a part of a story I knew. Why hadn't I chosen a longer passage of well-known verse instead? Even one of those childhood songs I used to sing for my company of simple freemen might have been better. . . .

"That notion of a sparrow's flight is found in Bede's writing," was what Wil said, "among the words that helped convert the first Christian king north of the Humber."

And he was right. I'd taken the story from a lesson about the conversion of the pagan king Eadwine. But I didn't have much time to feel surprised that he knew the text.

"Can you do it with the harp?" he was already asking. I had devised a plaintive little tune during my days of practice, and so I sang the words, with Wil listening intently.

"The first time was better," Wil pronounced when I was through, "but Osgar likes a singer. You'll use the harp."

The next evening Wil insisted I play my harp and sing the song in our camp for the first time.

"Our scop has something new for you tonight," Wil announced, and conversation quieted. Taking a deep breath, I plucked my first note—but then the beginning words of my song stuck in my throat and would not come. My fingers kept moving, and I played the tune through with my heart pounding hard enough to shake my whole body, and the taste of fear and failure rose bitterly in my mouth.

Like a cornered animal, I lifted my eyes and glanced around the circle of listening faces. The men were waiting, I saw. Simply waiting, not disappointed—not yet. *Mother used to listen to the scops who came to our hall like this: as if she simply hoped they would play well.* With determination I struck up my song anew. This time my words came with the music, and I offered Wil's men the hall, and the sparrow, and the storm.

There was no sound when my music died away, none of

the good-natured teasing that had followed the story of my journey with Wil, or my riddles. Only silence.

I had done my best, but it looked as if my performance had failed to interest them. I pressed a hand against my strings as I started to get up, not wanting to draw a single sound from them, hoping only to creep away into the dark and hide myself somewhere.

"That's as much as any of us can see, isn't it?" Kenelm spoke up gruffly. "Only the moments behind us, and ahead of us, like that sparrow in the hall."

I froze, seeing nods in the firelight and, unbelievably, one rough-faced man drawing the back of his huge hand across his eyes. I looked at Wil in amazement, but he didn't seem surprised. Somehow I had made the right choice.

Osgar still did not recognize me when Wil brought me back to his hall for the third time. "My scop will perform for your pleasure," Wil told him, and a look of bored politeness remained on Osgar's face until he saw that I intended to sing *and* play. Then his expression brightened.

This time I sang with no hesitation, and afterward Osgar raised his voice with the others in my praise. He gave me five silver pennies, leaving me astonished at my sudden wealth. Then Wil was called forward, and Osgar smiled and bowed.

"Bring your scop again, any time you come," he told my lord. And instead of returning to our bench, Wil was led by the steward to a seat at the high table.

I went back to my place at our smaller table with Wil's men. From there I could still see Wil talking with Osgar. They laughed together, and then, for just a moment, Wil's gaze found mine. His brief look told me he was happy with me and with what I had done, and with a sweet, distressing lurch, I found myself wishing he would never look away.

18

Into the Storm

Sometimes I think that those summer days between my first and second performances in Osgar's hall were like the sparrow's flight in the song I'd made. For a while, all pursuers and threats seemed distant. It was a space of existence, scarcely longer than a few wingbeats, spent in warmth and good company: out of the storm.

But Wil was still a man who'd lost his land, and whatever else I felt about him, I knew he was preparing to fight back. That night, following my performance, I was invited to attend a council meeting, and what I heard as I sat there quietly near the tent wall confirmed what I had guessed about Wil's former life in Eoforwic.

After Rægnald's invasion, Wil had gathered up a handful of surviving retainers faithful to him and ridden south on borrowed and stolen horses. Some of the Mercians who had intended to aid Eoforwic left their holdings in the care of their wives and servants and quietly came to join his camp, too. Kenelm was one of these. All of them, as far as I could tell, were bound together by their hatred of two people: Rægnald the Norse invader, and King Edward of Wessex.

There was rage in the voice of one former thane of Eoforwic who spoke up in the council circle that evening. "We sit here camped at Cirenceaster eating barley bread and drinking stale water while Rægnald prepares to take in all the harvest of our farmlands in a few weeks' time. He has our goods, our estates—the church has lost its gold and the minster library is at the Norsemen's mercy. And what does Edward do? What he has always done! He sits idle, strengthening his own fortresses, and leaves the English in the north to be Rægnald's slaves!"

"Why *do* we wait here?" This was Kenelm. "Friendship with Osgar will help our cause—you've told me that, Wil, but I still don't understand exactly how. Every week or so he feeds us better than we feed ourselves, but beyond that I hardly see—"

"We will talk about Osgar's usefulness tonight," Wil interrupted. His stern tone reminded everyone in the circle that he was a large, strong man with the kind of battle experience that would serve him well in a brawl. Kenelm took a step back, although Wil had uttered no threat or warning, and I settled deeper into my shadowy spot to hear what our leader would say next.

"In Gleawceastershire loyalty to Edward runs shallower than in most other parts of his kingdom. The Lady of the Mercians and Aldorman Ethelred are buried there; people here remember them. I have even heard"—Wil looked grim—"that Edward tried to take Lady Æthelflæd's daughter on the very day of the lady's burial, and that the Mercians in Gleawceaster prevented it for Æthelflæd's sake.

"So in Gleawceaster we have friends who bring pledges of loyalty," he continued, "who would fight against Rægnald, in spite of King Edward's neglect of Northumbria."

"But we have tried this before, Wil, in Lunden," called out another of the Northumbrian thanes, "and Edward spoiled all our Mercian alliances simply by taking the girl. . . ."

It was chilling to hear my true name spoken among my new companions. Wil pounded his fist against his thigh. "Ælfwyn of Mercia was a friend to Eoforwic, and none of us was there to stop King Edward when he finally took her by force at Christmastide last!" He scowled. "We should all feel as guilty about that as do the Mercian thanes who visit my tent, and who sometimes even stay"—he looked pointedly at Kenelm—"hoping to find a way to make right the quarrels and distrust that ruptured our friendships after the lady's daughter was taken. We should have prevented Edward from taking her at all costs. We should have acknowledged to each other, and to Ælfwyn, that it was her blood—her mother's memory living in her—that kept us together as long as she was in Mercia." Wil paused a moment, then went on in a quieter voice. "I have had word from Dunstan. No one can say where the girl is. Even the noblewoman who went into Wessex as her companion does not know what Edward has done with her now. She can't be found in Wintanceaster, we know. She may be dead." Fiercely, he looked around the circle of faces. "Friends, what we begin at Cirenceaster, we will finish, unlike our attempt last year. And we will do it for the sake of Lady Ælfwyn, as much as for our own cause."

It was clear that for Wil, Ælfwyn of Mercia had become a regretful memory around which to rally a movement against my uncle. Fascinated, I moved a little closer into the circle.

"Let me tell you what I learned tonight from another visitor in Osgar's hall—one who came especially to give me this message," Wil continued. "The thing we have been waiting for—the possibility that brought us to Cirenceaster as summer began—has happened. King Edward's court will travel here in a fortnight."

Suddenly the haven I'd made for myself in Wil's camp vanished. A murmur ran around the council circle. Wil kept speaking.

"Osgar, who is Edward's loyal thane, will host a great feast to welcome the king and those who come with him. And he will invite us, the landless northerners, hoping we will admire his friendship with King Edward and agree to join his house-band. Osgar will also be pleased to have our scop play for Edward that night, and when Widsith plays . . ."

I didn't hear what he said next. Wil wanted me to play for Uncle Edward in Osgar's hall. If I hadn't been terrified, I would have laughed out loud.

". . . the only way to make him act on behalf of English

people in the north. We have friends who will gather outside
the hall, and there will be enough of us inside to hold the
king at Cirenceaster until he sends an army to Eoforwic to
drive back the Norse!"

The talk swelled up again, and I crouched in my dark corner unnoticed. In Lunden we had verged on treason when
we'd mustered Mercian arms and men without Edward's
consent. But to hold the king by force in Cirenceaster . . . it
was a desperate act, and it could very likely mean the death
of every person in this tent tonight.

"Widsith!" Wil had skirted the crowd to find me. "The
song for the royal visit—I want it to be something no one
has heard before. Our friends will be gathering while you
entertain, you see? And every eye and ear in the hall must
be fixed on you. Do you know such a poem?"

I looked at Wil, who fairly brimmed with all the force of
his plans. Wil, whose opinion I'd come to cherish, and whose
idea was terribly dangerous for reasons he could never guess.
What in the name of all creation should I say?

"I . . . I think maybe I can make one," I heard myself answer.

19

JUDITH

THEY'D GIVEN ME FOURTEEN DAYS TO COMPOSE A POEM THAT would distract King Edward and his men while Wil's thanes surrounded them. I suppose I could have run away right then, but where? At the very least I would have both Edward's and Wilfrid's men looking for me, for Wil would not easily let me go now that I knew his plans. I would be alone again, and I knew now how vulnerable that made me. I would be clinging to a warhorse I could hardly ride as I galloped away . . . no, I would stay at Cirenceaster, and try to discover what I had to do.

For a day Wil left me alone, but then he came asking about what I was planning to sing. "A poem this time, Widsith?" he said in a tone that was half-question, half-request.

Yes, I assured him, though my heart was racing as I said it. I had decided to use the story of a hero, I said to Wil: a tale I'd learned in Latin, although my poem would be in English.

This news seemed to satisfy him, for he pressed me no further, and when I asked for parchment and something to write with, he sent Kenelm to the market in Cirenceaster to get them for me. When I asked for a quiet place, a table, and a rushlight for nighttime writing, I was given those as well. When I asked if there was any way I could see a Bible, Wil gave a snort of astonishment, but two days later I found a fine leather-bound Vulgate on my table. I worried that he had robbed a monastery.

Still, I needed that Bible, and I opened it to the Book of Judith. There were the lines I'd read with Grimbald and Mother that last day, before she rode to Tameworthig. My eyes raced over the words. Judith the valiant Israelite widow, by herself deceiving and beheading Holofernes the Assyrian general, and then rallying her people to drive off the entire invading army. Slowly I began to translate the lines from Latin into English—into English poetry.

> *Now I wish to urge each man among you,*
> *Burgh-dwellers and shield-warriors,*
> *To ready yourselves with haste for battle.*

My pen moved more and more confidently as I wrote. Judith's people had faced an enemy as fierce as the Danish jarls who came raiding into Mercia—as fierce as the Norsemen who had overrun Eoforwic. I could put such terrors into English words! And above all there was Judith, the

hero. In my lifetime I had known only one woman as force-
ful as Judith. I was beginning to believe I could write about
her, too.

Days passed. My back ached from bending over the book
and my pages. My eyes burned from peering in sunlight and
through smoky rushlight alike at the words I wrote. The fingers of my writing hand were stained with ink again for the
first time since I'd left Lunden, and it felt right, somehow, to
see it. Still, each time I sat down to my work, I could feel my
stomach churning with the danger of what I had agreed to
do, and with worry for my friends. Wil was making a desperate attempt of his own, but he had no idea what he had
risked by including me in his plans.

I should leave, I told myself at least ten times each day as
I wrote. And still I stayed in Wil's camp, working toward his
foolish, dangerous goal. What was really keeping me there?
Weakness, perhaps. I was used to the regular food, and going
to my bed in the same place each night. At last I had duties
here that occupied all my time. These things made the dan-
gers seem more distant than they really were, I think. But
there was something more: Wil's company, the sight of his
cross face in the morning when he came from an argument
with his advisers to ask me how the writing progressed, the
approving hand he laid on my shoulder when I sang well in
the evening. It was harder and harder for me to think of not
seeing and feeling and hearing him each day. Stupidly, nec-
essarily, I stayed in his camp.

◆ ◆ ◆

It didn't help at all when King Edward came to Cirenceaster three days earlier than anyone expected. I had run out of ink on the afternoon it happened, and Wil had sent me to the market by myself. "To keep you from shriveling into a blind and crooked old man—you've been bent over that poem too long," he told me. After I bought my ink, I accidentally tipped the little clay pot the merchant had handed to me and dribbled a stream of the acidic liquid across my wrist. Before I was clear of the *tun* walls I'd had to stop, put down the pot, and scrub at the stinging stain with my sleeve. My fingers were tough, used to the bite of ink. The skin farther up my arm was not.

Then I heard the shouting.

I sometimes wonder if things would have been different had I not spilled the ink in the market that day.

I saw the royal guards first, and Uncle Edward riding with Æthelstan beside him. In the next seconds I caught sight of the women riding in the first of a sumptuous train of wagons behind the king. There was the queen, Eadgifu—Edward's third wife and Æthelstan's stepmother, whom I had seen but never spoken with in Wintanceaster. I was already raising an arm to cover my face, but when I saw who sat beside the queen, I turned, scooped up my pot of ink, and ran. It was Gytha. And alongside the queen's wagon, on a splendid warhorse that could only have been a gift from King Edward's own stables, rode Aldwulf, Earl of East Anglia.

✦ ✦ ✦

"They've all come," said Kenelm that night. "The king and queen, and their youngest son and daughter, and Lord Æthelstan—"

"And a beauty with hair red as fire, I've heard," laughed another man.

"She's promised to old Aldwulf," said the stocky thane who sat closest to my little table, "so forget about that lovely face."

So Gytha was promised to Aldwulf. He had always wanted her loveliness, and now he could have it, along with my uncle's favor. I hadn't guessed that my leaving Wintanceaster might affect my friend that way. Gytha—she'd had no choice.

"Widsith, are you well?" It was Wil, leaning over my table. "I need you for tomorrow night, boy." He looked at my pages anxiously. "Osgar's sent word that he'll welcome Edward with a feast tomorrow evening. Our allies will be ready. Will you be prepared?"

I gazed at my writing. The poem was nearly done, but how could I learn the lines by heart in such a short time? I raised my eyes to Wil's, saw what he needed me to say.

"I'll be ready," I lied.

When Wil had gone, I put my head down on my arms. My mother had been Lady Æthelflæd, praised and honored by her people. She had known how to speak with men, how best to quell enemies and please friends. She would have known what to do now, but she wasn't here to tell me.

After a moment I made myself sit up. I dipped my pen and set to work writing the last lines of my poem.

The enemy had lost their leader.

> *Distraught in mind,*
> *They threw down their weapons, weary-hearted,*
> *Hastened away in flight . . .*

When the poem was done, I sat staring at my rushlight. The flame drank up the last of the oil, then slowly consumed the wick until it disappeared into the empty bowl that held it.

There had been a night, three years ago, when word came to Lunden that my mother had taken a party into Wales to avenge the death of a slain abbot called Ecgberht who had been dear to her. I'd thought of Judith then, as I listened to Edith tell me how Mother broke across the Welsh dyke and took thirty-four prisoners captive, including the wife of the offending king. *"Avenge now, mighty Lord, that which is so grievously in my mind, so hot in my heart."* Those were Judith's words, but they might just as well have been my mother's.

Judith. Æthelflæd. Would my audience understand? And would I really be able to stand and sing in front of Edward, Æthelstan—all the members of the traveling court—without giving myself away and imperiling Wil? I bit at a fingernail, grinding it to the quick.

But maybe there was another possibility—one person I could seek out for help now, when I most needed it. But to go and ask might well be the most dangerous thing I could possibly do.

20

HOT BLOOD

QUIETLY THE NEXT MORNING I LEFT CAMP AND, TROTTING along on foot in the predawn light, made my way into the burgh. A wattled fence marked the edge of Osgar's properties in Cirenceaster, and I sat down with my back against it until I saw servants beginning to bustle around the main buildings.

"You have royal guests today," I said to a young serving woman who came to fling the contents of a wooden pail over the fence and into the road. She twitched her thick plait of hair back over her shoulder.

"You'd think there were twice as many of them, with all the work they've made for us." She pursed her lips peevishly. "The king and a few others were ready for their breakfast half an hour before the kitchens had planned, but some of the ladies are only just waking."

"That beauty with the red hair who rode with the queen yesterday . . ."

"Still in her chamber. Only just awake, I'd guess." The

woman's eyes narrowed. "You're not the first to ask about her, boy. She's promised to Aldwulf, so you can tell your master, whoever he is, that she's—"

"My master's not wooing the lady. I was called here to play for her, whenever she wants me." I flipped back the cover of my satchel to show the woman the harp I carried inside. "From what you tell me, I suppose I'll have a long wait."

The serving woman planted the bucket on one hip and stared at me. "You're that boy scop who played in the hall, aren't you?" she asked.

"Mmm." I nodded.

"Who sent you to wait here?"

"Someone in Lord Osgar's household." I shrugged. "They said to come for the lady's pleasure, should she need entertainment this morning."

The woman wrinkled her brow. "Entertainment this morning? Well, I'll tell them you're here." She tromped back toward the busy grounds, and I settled down to wait some more. *Please let Gytha be as curious as ever. Let her wonder about a scop sitting outside the fence.*

They came to fetch me to Gytha's chamber after just one peal of midmorning bells. A door and a window were open in her room, but the other windows remained shuttered to preserve cool air inside. I slipped gratefully into a shadow as soon as I crossed Gytha's threshold.

"Who are you?" *Her voice!* She was sitting in the shadows, too, I could dimly make out as my eyes adjusted to the indoor light. A lump filled my throat at the sight of my friend.

"A scop, sent to play for you, Lady," I said huskily.

"You say Osgar sent you. The servants here have heard nothing of that." I cleared my throat, steadied my voice.

"They told you it was Osgar?" I pretended to be surprised, then changed my lie, hoping fervently she would believe what I said. "Oh, no, my lady. My master is another of the lord's guests, who has pledged my skill to the service of Lord Osgar and all his household. My own master sent me."

For the space of a few breaths she and I and the two serving women who were with her stayed perfectly still. *She will throw me out, or have me seized and taken away. Such a stupid thing to come here, to risk so much just to see Gytha and trade a few words with her. . . .*

"It's all right," Gytha said at last to the women standing by. "He can stay." With a nod to the other servant, one of the women slipped through the door. The remaining woman settled herself on a stool in the corner, keeping her eyes on the two of us. I began to fumble with my satchel. This wasn't going to be easy.

"I don't know if I really want music this morning, boy," came Gytha's voice again as I rested the harp against my arm and chest. She sounded very tired. "Our journey only ended yesterday," she explained. "Rest, not entertainment, was what I had in mind."

It was hard to make myself speak up again, but I had to. "I . . . I don't have to sing, nor must I play, Lady. I have some words a traveler might appreciate, though." *Would she say yes?*

"Well, yes then. Tell them to me, young scop."

I lowered my harp onto the floor and clasped my hands in front of me. *Let her remember our lessons on Bede. Let her see that no ordinary scop would know this tale.* "This present life," I said softly, "is such a thing as when you sit a-feasting with aldermen and thanes in wintertime, the fire burning in the hall, the rains and storms and snows outside." I told her about the sparrow, the hall, the moment of flight. I was afraid to look at her while I recited, but when I fell silent again, and I knew a quaver in my voice could not betray me, I did look up and try to see her reaction.

"A storm outside the hall," Gytha murmured. "All the bird knows for certain is what it can see before and behind it for the moment it flies beneath the roof's shelter." She stood up. "An odd entertainment for a summer's morning, scop, but it was well spoken," she said flatly. She turned to the serving woman in the corner. "Will you go and ask the earl if we may reward the boy with a few coins?" The woman hesitated; it was a strange request. Surely a noblewoman like Gytha would have had some money about her own person.

"Will you go?" Gytha's voice was sharper this time, and the woman quickly got up and went out. As soon as she had gone, Gytha flew across the room and drew the cloth curtain across the door.

"*Ælfwyn!*" she hissed, catching me in a crushing embrace. "Hair lopped off, dirty boy's clothes, but Ælfwyn, underneath, spouting our childhood lessons. Where have you been!" she demanded in my ear.

"Hiding," I whispered back, tears blinding me, "on the road. Here. They think I'm a boy scop. I play for Lord Osgar sometimes. I . . ." There was too much to tell her, and no time to say it.

"What can I do?" she said, holding me out at arm's length and searching my face. "They're still looking for you, you know. The king thinks that his enemies took you and will try to use you against him. He's worried about the alliances your mother once ensured for him."

"Is your marriage to Aldwulf meant to ensure *that* friendship, at least?"

Gytha held up her hands helplessly. "Aldwulf wanted me. Everyone thought he would shout betrayal and treachery when you disappeared. Instead, he asked for my hand, as if that would satisfy him as much as wedding the king's own niece." She grimaced, fighting her own tears. "Maybe I should have run, like you, Wyn. But I thought maybe"—she caught her breath in a sob and embraced me again—"maybe I could have a child, an heir for my family's lands. Aldwulf will be made aldorman of East Anglia, I'm told. I'm a Danish raider's bastard, everyone knows, but now my child could have as much honor in Wessex as my grandfather once had in Mercia." All at once she gripped me by the shoulders. "They'll be coming back in a minute, Wyn. What do you want me to do for you? Tell me what I can do!"

"They want me to play for the king at the feast this evening," I told her. "I don't see how I can stay—"

"Edward would recognize you, just as I did." Gytha was already running to a chest in the corner of her room, pulling out clothing: a dress, metal ornaments, fine leather shoes, a wimple and veil.

"There's one serving woman I trust," Gytha said as she rushed back to me, her arms full of clothes. "The two of us can hide you in our company—why would anyone look for you in the king's own household? We're going east to Aldwulf's burgh when we leave Cirenceaster. We'll get word to Mother, so she can find some friend along the way who can shelter you." A sound of voices and footsteps came through the door hanging. "It's Aldwulf, coming with the servant!" she whispered frantically, shoving the clothes into my satchel as I grabbed it from the floor. "He might know you, as I did! Go out the far window, Wyn, he's coming the other way!" I was already scrambling over the sill, trying not to rattle the open shutters. I dropped to the ground, then straightened up as quickly as I could. I had come out fast enough that perhaps no one had noticed me. Now I had to look as if I were just passing by.

"Come back before tonight," came Gytha's voice, barely audible. "I'll do whatever I can, Wyn."

I walked briskly until another building hid me from Gytha's quarters, and then I made myself slow down. I more than half expected to hear the sound of feet and voices pursuing me—my back prickled with the anticipation of a chase—but none came. Gytha had explained it all somehow.

Farther from Osgar's grounds I began to relax a little. If I could find some place to change, I could creep back and hide there just as Gytha had suggested. No one would look for the boy scop in women's dress. No one would look for Ælfwyn in plain sight of my uncle. I felt the soft bulge of the clothes in the satchel under my arm and beneath it the unyielding circle of my harp.

But what about Wil? I couldn't stay, couldn't be part of his plan. But he'd think I'd betrayed him.

"Where're you going, boy?" Suddenly my left arm was gripped painfully from behind and I was shoved off the street, around a corner, and pinned up against the wall of an unused shed. I twisted around, trying to see who held me. Wil, sweat dripping from his red face, breathing as if he'd been running, glared at me. "We've been looking all over the burgh for you," he said, his voice low. "Someone heard from a slave that you'd gone to where the king and his company slept. Did you?" Wil kept my arm in his unyielding grip.

"I—I finished the poem last night," I stammered. "I just came into the burgh this morning to—to—"

"To what?" Wil demanded quietly. His face was an unreadable mask, but there was no mistaking the menace in his tone. I cringed beside him. "You've been sneaking in shadows, listening to our private talk in camp. Did you come here to tell someone what you've heard?"

"No! No!" I protested. He was holding me so tightly that I was afraid he'd feel my softer flesh and fine bones, and discover my girl's body inside the boy's clothes. "I only gave your greetings to the red-haired lady! Told her you'd sent me as a favor this morning, to cheer her after her journey! I said I'd be performing at the feast tonight, but nothing more! That's all I said!"

Suddenly Wil's fingers opened, and I staggered backward and tripped over a hump in the ground at the side of the road. He was coming for me again, and I rolled to one side, desperate to avoid his reach. His hand closed on my wrist.

And then he was pulling me up gently, helping me to my feet.

"Of course that's all you said," he mumbled. "I'm sorry." He dropped my wrist and stood there, staring at his own empty hands. "She's a beautiful woman, I've heard." He shook his head. "I should have known it was only a young man's hot blood drawing you out of our camp. But going after a noblewoman betrothed to Edward's staunchest ally? I didn't guess that."

He thinks I followed Gytha's fair face. For the moment Wil's steadying voice was enough to calm my thumping heart a little. Yes, let him believe that his scop had behaved foolishly, but not treacherously.

I would stay here with him for another minute or two. Then I'd think of some way to slip away, find somewhere to change my clothes and veil my face, and then back to Gytha—she'd be watching for me.

"We've been looking all over the burgh for you," Wil repeated woodenly. "I'm sorry, boy. I didn't mean to be rough. I was beginning to think you might be fated to desert me."

He covered his face with one hand. "My lands are gone, and my title. The people who once trusted me to protect them now live in Rægnald's grip. Death took my wife when she tried to give me a child. And when I learned that King Edward had taken his niece who'd been my ally—that he'd killed her, most likely—it seemed that nothing I wanted was mine to keep." Wil's dark eyes found mine. "Are you Mercian, boy? I never asked. . . ." What could it hurt to tell the truth?

"I am."

"Then you lost Lady Ælfwyn, too"—he pulled me to him

in a rough embrace—"as well as your family, you said. Maybe between us we've had our share of misfortune already."

"Wil!" It was Kenelm, striding toward us. "So you found the little wretch, and welcomed him back like a long-lost son, I see." Wil released me, and Kenelm shook me playfully by the shoulders. "He was shouting all over the camp when we found you missing, first cursing your name and your profession, then swearing Osgar's men had somehow taken you away. I thought you said you'd beat the whelp if we discovered him wandering in the burgh," he said, turning back to Wil.

"If Widsith does well in the hall tonight, I won't," Wil muttered.

"Too soft!" Kenelm snorted. "But he's always favored you, boy. 'Talent, but no training,' was what he said when we heard you that first night in Osgar's hall, and the next thing we knew, there you were in our camp having lessons from him. Is that why you brought him home, Wil? You wanted a disciple?"

"We were both travelers," Wil replied simply. "We started traveling together."

Kenelm didn't press him further. "I'll find the others if you want to go back to camp," he told Wil. The two of them started for the road.

"Are you coming, Widsith?" Wil called back.

I remembered Gytha clinging to me. *"I'll do whatever I*

can, Wyn." How could I choose between these two evils? To stay with Wil any longer was an act of treason against my uncle. But if I escaped with Gytha I'd be leaving Wil, betraying him.

Wil's dark eyes were watching me. I met his gaze, held it.

"Yes, I'm coming."

21

LAST WORDS

I SPENT THE AFTERNOON GOING OVER MY SHEETS OF PARCHment, feeling more and more sick at heart. The threat of violence in the hall loomed even closer, driving the words of my poem out of my head.

I sat in the red tent and through the opening I watched my companions dress themselves for the feast. They strapped their weapons subtly along their limbs or beneath the bright tunics they pulled over close-fitting body armor. Some of the horses' saddles would bear concealed battle axes and short swords, too, in case the evening ended in failure and a fighting retreat. The men laughed and talked as they got ready. I stared at the lines I'd scrawled on my pages, but mostly I thought about fighting in close quarters, and the kinds of death that might come from it. When no one was watching, I wedged my mother's knife beneath my belt. Soon the sun had sunk low in the sky.

"Widsith!" It was Kenelm, hair trimmed back, and wearing a yellow garment I'd never seen before. "Your horse is saddled and waiting," he said as he came into the tent. "Later tonight we may need to let one of the others ride him, and you can ride behind me . . . but look at you, boy! You look just the way you did when I found you after you scuffled in the dirt with Wil! This is a royal feast, little idiot! Will you wash your hands and face at least, before we go?"

Hopelessly, I nodded. I would go with clean hands and face to greet disaster.

Wil rode up while I was washing and looked me over. "Should have got you some new clothes in the burgh today. The rest of us are dressed to see the king."

New clothes. This was all he was worried about? My companions were on their way to a royal feast, hardly mentioning that they intended to hold the king of all English Britain hostage. . . .

"I'll wait outside the hall," I told him, feeling miserable, "until it's time for me to sing." The longer I could keep out of King Edward's sight the better for Wil. Wil cocked his head, weighing what I'd said.

"All right. Where's your harp, boy?" I pointed to where my satchel lay beside my writing table. "Well, go get it, and mount up!" Wil put his heels into his horse's sides and galloped off. I gave the back of my neck a last scrub with my rag and then hesitated briefly before walking over to scoop up my bag. No one saw me grab the sheaf of parchment from the table and shove it in under the flap of the satchel.

I wanted the few minutes' ride into Cirenceaster to last a hundred times longer than it did. "Keep up, Widsith!" they kept calling to me as I lagged at the back of the party. All twenty-three men in camp had come this time. No horses had been left behind, and the most valuable things from camp that could be carried discreetly were strapped to the saddles. All the fires were out. We could leave and not come back, if we had to.

Where was the solution that would end this mad plan? I wondered as I jounced in the saddle, riding even more poorly than usual, and feeling not at all eager to reach our destination. Mother would have hated what was going to happen tonight in Osgar's hall. She would have found a way to change it.

No answers had come to me before we were all dismounting at the stables. The stable hands were ready for us, knowing that Wil always grandly rode the short distance to the feasts to show honor to his host. Against all my wishes, I found myself standing by the doors of the hall as our men went in. It was too warm a night for the old cloak I'd thrown over my clothes, but I'd felt the need to hide them, after so many complaints.

"You stand here, boy," said Wil, who was the last to enter, apart from me. "I'll send the steward to you." Then he leaned closer to whisper, "Don't make a sound, no matter what you hear or see out in the yard, understand?"

Eyes wide, I nodded.

Then he grinned. "Good luck, Widsith. I hope your verse is finer than that costume of yours. Hey, are you scared, boy?" He must have noticed the terror on my face at last. "Widsith, you're a good scop. The clothes won't matter." He touched my smooth jaw. "And you've a fair face, as pretty as a girl's, the men sometimes say." He chucked me roughly under the chin. "I'll kiss you myself," he joshed, "to prove that folk will care more about those big eyes of yours than anything you're wearing." And then he did kiss me, a friend's honorable salute on the cheek. "Sing well, boy." He disappeared inside.

Alone, I stood in the shadows beside the doorway, watching the guests throng past, still feeling the brush of Wil's beard against my skin, his lips against my cheek. Did he really need me in order to carry out the rest of his plan? There was terrible risk in showing myself to Edward, and even more in letting him hear my voice, as my encounter with Gytha had proven. But Wil—how could he proceed if his scop didn't appear? How could I leave him? My feet didn't move.

Where was the steward Wil had promised to send? I could hear a large party approaching the door, and as they came into sight I scuttled around the corner of the building and flattened myself against the wall. It was Osgar, I saw as I peered sideways and caught a glimpse of the group, Osgar walking in with King Edward and the rest of the royal visitors—a party of twenty or more altogether. They paused at the entrance—I could hear their loud talking grow quieter.

"Greetings, King Edward," said the steward (he must have bowed very low, for his voice seemed to come from somewhere near the ground). "You honor us with this visit."

"You have our thanks," came the king's voice—it chilled me to hear him so close, after so many weeks spent running and skulking in disguise. I shrank a little closer to the wall, hearing the king murmur to someone near him. Footsteps. A jingle of money.

"Accept this token of our gratitude," I heard Æthelstan say, his words accompanied by the clink of silver coins being placed in the steward's hands. The steward began to elaborately acknowledge King Edward's generosity, but Osgar cut him off.

"All our other guests have arrived?" Osgar wanted to know.

"Yes, my lord."

"And the entertainers?"

"Your scop waits at the foot of the high table. I've come to fetch the northerners' scop—they said he was waiting outside."

"Find him, then," Osgar replied curtly. Then in a far more obsequious tone, he added, "Welcome to my hall, King Edward."

I heard the group walk inside. Then the steward's voice

came again, with no hint of obeisance anymore. "The boy was supposed to be here. Eomer!" he shouted into the hall. Footsteps came running. "I need the young scop who came to play. Find him for me."

"Sir, they are waiting for me to help carry the roast boar!"

There was a little pause. "Well, curse him, then," the steward said flatly. "Let the lad make his own way into the hall, and have a beating from his master if he fails to show his face. Osgar's own scop can play twice, if he has to."

Then I heard the coins rattle again—the steward must be dropping them into a purse that hung from his belt. "A handful of silver for me. Gold for Osgar, no doubt," the man muttered. "The king pays his supporters well." With a scurry and a swish of garments, he was gone.

I started breathing again, my mind racing. The steward would not come looking for me again. So I could go, and no one would seek me out, before the feast's end. *"He wasn't yet dead—not entirely lifeless."* The words began repeating over and over in my head; it was a line from the poem, one of the phrases I'd been trying to memorize all afternoon. *"He wasn't yet dead—"*

I wasn't yet dead. I should go, now! Winter was in the stable—was there any way to get to him without being seen and questioned? Gytha's quarters were nearby . . . but she was in the hall with the rest of them.

I peered around the corner. The feast had begun, and as far as I could tell it was richer than anything I'd seen in Osgar's hall before. Servants carried whole roasted animals on scrubbed boards, honey cakes, fresh and salted fish, cheeses, and ale, and even wine from across the sea poured into graceful long-necked flagons of colored glass.

"You'd better go," I whispered to myself, but instead I closed my eyes, leaned my back against the wall, and let the smells and sounds of the celebration wash out over me.

The poem was in my head again, words spoken by the heroine Judith to her people before battle. *"Your enemies are sentenced to death, and you will have honor, glory in the battle, just as the mighty Lord has shown you by my hand."*

Your enemies are sentenced to death. I wasn't even sure who my real enemies were. My uncle, who had taken me out of Mercia by force, but who had also helped defend Mercia against Danish raiders for years? Wilfrid, who had taken in, taught, and cared for a wandering boy, but who would stop at nothing—even rebellion against King Edward—to reclaim his lands?

English people everywhere had lost much to invaders. I remembered the miller's deserted burgh, Gytha's grandfather who had lost first his family and finally his life to the Danes. Wil's losses were also great, and he was a good man. How could I leave him? But Wil planned to overpower the very man most capable of preserving English lands ... would weakening Edward's power really save Eoforwic?

Mother would have hated it. All of it. I backed around the corner to my hiding place again. Without thought, my hands reached into my satchel and pulled out the pages I'd stuffed on top. Beneath them was the wad of clothing Gytha had given me. *After a lifetime of making allies out of enemies, Mother might have found a way.* I loosened the clasp of my cloak, let it fall from my shoulders. *"We were both travelers."* The crush of Wil's embrace. *"Are you coming, Widsith?"* I fumbled with my clothes, pulled light folds of a woman's linen tunic over my head, then the heavier cloth of the overgown. *Gytha gripping me by the shoulders. "Maybe I could have a child, an heir for my family's lands."* I secured the clasp of the fine girdle Gytha had given me, then the clasp of my own cloak at my neck again. Shoving my sheathed dagger beneath the girdle, I drew the cloak around me and pulled up the hood, hiding my face.

I would run. Wearing Gytha's dress, I would become a woman again—I'd stop being Widsith just long enough to get out of Cirenceaster. Then, a few miles down the road, I would turn myself back into a boy scop and flee as far from both Edward and Wil as possible. I held my breath as the last servants entered the hall, and then the doors were pushed shut. Inside, the feasters quieted a little, and the first scop began to sing.

Something moved at the edge of the courtyard. I scooped up my handful of pages, my harp, and the satchel stuffed full of Widsith's leathers, and cowered back against the wall. I would need to stay hidden until the way was clear for me to leave. Out in the yard the royal guards and the king's own men stood at intervals, covering the center of the yard. I squinted. They looked settled, a little sleepy, even. But hadn't something just moved out there in the dark?

The thudding sound of something hard against human flesh froze me where I crouched. Dark figures had come up around the royal guards and Osgar's own men, and these shapes now surrounded everyone who had been keeping watch outside the hall. *"Don't make a sound, no matter what you hear or see"*—that's what Wil had said. I bit my lips together to keep from screaming as the shadows struck, silencing the guards with blows and quick slashes, muffling any cries with their hands or wads of cloth.

Two struggling bodies rolled toward my corner and slammed into me, throwing me to the ground and hurling my things out into the darkness. Half-blinded by my hood, I clutched for the strap of my satchel with one hand, then caught at my harpstrings just as a booted foot came crashing down on the frame, trapping and bruising my fingers. In the space of ten breaths every one of the king's and Osgar's men was down, some of them unquestionably dead.

I sprawled there, gasping, in the open. One of the figures stepped close to me, lifted me swiftly to my feet, and raised a hand toward my mouth. I would have screamed then, but the person only placed his fingers upon my lips and gripped my shoulder hard. I forced myself to stand quietly, my broken harp dangling from one battered hand.

"Are you the scop?" the figure hissed. Terrified, I nodded,

certain I'd be treated no better than the felled guards if I said no. After a moment my captor pushed me back to stand on one side of the hall doorway, then stepped to the other side of the door himself. "They told me you'd be waiting by the door," he muttered. "Didn't mean to knock you down."

I stood there, muffled and hooded in my cloak, injured fingers throbbing. A little light escaped through the cracks around the doorjamb, and I saw the face of the man who'd picked me up. It was Dunstan.

What twisted fortune had brought him to my side?

"They're almost ready for you, scop," he murmured. He was wearing leather armor and ring mail, which made him look very much like any other thane from Wil's camp. He and the men who had come with him must be the supporters from around Gleawceastershire of whom Wil had spoken. "I'll walk in with you," Dunstan said softly, drawing his cloak close around him to hide his armor and sword, "and hang back while you play. When we see that they are all listening, your leader and I will move to take the king. Then you must watch out for yourself. Get away from the center of the room. It'll be safer by the walls."

All I could do was nod. Shuddering, I pulled my own cloak even tighter over my woman's clothing. Somehow no one, not even Dunstan, had glimpsed the fine gown underneath, but little good that would do me a few moments from now. Unless I could find another chance to escape, I would have to enter the hall.

Furtively, I glanced around the yard as Dunstan's men busied themselves dragging off and concealing the fallen sentries. Something on the ground caught the light from the crack between the hall doors. Swiftly I grabbed the object and resumed my stance.

A silver penny—the busy steward must have missed his purse, and the servants bustling past afterward had trodden it into the ground. If I did ever manage to get away, I'd need this money, I thought, looking at King Edward's profile on the face of the coin. The words EDWARD REX shone out plainly—it was a new penny, barely worn. Gingerly, I turned the disk over with my bruised fingers, then felt every muscle go taut as I read the name of the mint-town: EOFORWIC.

Eoforwic? If they were minting English money in Eofor-wic, that must mean . . . Edward already had some agreement with Rægnald—some treaty that would soon be well known, I guessed, remembering the king's carefree use of this coin. Suddenly I thought of Wil, whose plan was to force the king to send an army to Eoforwic against the Norse. But King Edward had not ignored Rægnald, he had bent him to his own purposes somehow! And if Edward had already won Rægnald's fealty, then Wil's actions would not save Northumbria tonight. They would only condemn him to death.

I had to tell Wil somehow, I thought, clutching the coin. In a moment Osgar's servants would let me go into the hall . . . and I would go in, I resolved. I would walk to the high table, and try to say or do something, I didn't know what—anything to save Wil and my friends.

Shouts and cheers had begun to fill the hall on the other side of the doors. I jumped in panic as the doors swung inward, and one of Osgar's serving people gestured to show me that I should step inside. *This is madness. Dressed as a woman, all my words blown away*— But I had made up my mind. Dunstan kept close by my side as I entered the hall, then he backed into the shadows at the wall. I waited as the doors closed behind me. The bright clothing of feasters surrounded me. So many faces, and every one of them seemed strange to my frightened eyes.

But there was Osgar, at the high table. And Edward beside him, his face haggard, his expression inscrutable. Numbly I recognized Edward's queen, Eadgifu, and then found Aldwulf. The old fighter looked confused. Gytha beside him seemed stricken—she looked as if she might be sick.

"Thane," Osgar demanded in a loud voice, addressing Wil, "is this the boy scop you brought before? Call him forward. My guests are expecting entertainment, a song. . . ."

The blood was rushing to my face, but before Wil had to summon me, my feet began to step toward the high table again. Through the tunnel of my hood I saw Wil's eyes glittering at me. Perhaps he noticed that I carried no harp, for he scowled, then bent and whispered to Kenelm, who sat beside him.

I saw the stool where a scop should sit to sing and play. Well, I thought, clutching my cloak around me and coming to a halt beside it, this scop would stand instead. And say— what? My mouth was dry. My hand pulsed more and more painfully where it hung by my side, gripping the penny.

"Listen!" The word burst from my throat. Everyone was staring at the little hooded scop who spoke so abruptly. Wil sat forward. I ran my tongue over parched lips, then struggled on. "I have heard tell that in Gleawceastershire people remember Æthelflæd, Lady of the Mercians." Wil's eyes were blazing now, but Edward still sat, impassive. "So tonight I wanted to sing you verses, composed in Lady Æthelflæd's honor. . . ." My voice was barely strong enough to be heard beyond the high table, but Mother's name had caught everyone in the room by surprise.

Everyone but Wil. He must have seen how nervous I was and decided not to wait for me. He signaled to his men, for all at once I saw Kenelm drawing his short sword. Cries erupted all around the hall as he and the others from Wil's camp scrambled from their places and threw themselves at the thanes nearest the king. Wil seized Edward's arm and produced a dagger. Æthelstan, wielding only the little knife he'd brought for eating, lunged forward to grapple with Wil. The queen was screaming. Osgar was on his feet, enraged, calling for his own guards. But when I turned to look behind me, I saw Dunstan shoving open the doors and his renegades filling the doorway.

"Stop," I whispered, forgotten in the middle of the hall. Æthelstan was reaching for Wil's throat with one bloodied hand. Aldwulf, shoving Gytha behind him, grabbed at Kenelm's bright tunic with one hand and gripped his sword arm with the other.

"Stop! You have to stop!" I screamed, but still no one heard.

The benches were emptying as guests ran, a few going to the king's aid, most rushing for the doors, where Dunstan and his cohort waited with weapons drawn. Suddenly I saw the way to the high table clear in front of me. *They'll listen if I'm closer, if I can just make them hear me!* I dashed forward, flung my weight onto the table, and swung my legs up. In another moment I was on my feet, standing only an arm's length away from Wil and Uncle Edward. I tore at the brooch beneath my chin, ripping it free, and let my cloak drop from my shoulders.

"Listen!" I howled down from the tabletop. "Listen to me! I have something to say!"

Maybe it was my voice, ringing with a scop's strength from that height. Maybe it was the borrowed dress, a rich gown of light blue wool, revealed like a bright piece of sky in front of their eyes. The fighters stopped, let their hands drop, took a few steps back, gaping at me.

"Who are you?"

It was Wil who asked, and when I looked at him, I flinched away from his expression. *He sees Widsith's face atop a woman's body.* I knew Wil must be thinking of everything he had said to me, of everything he had revealed, realizing how much I had concealed. The look of peevish affection he'd shown me ever since I came into his camp had disappeared completely.

"She is Ælfwyn of Mercia," King Edward answered, startling every other person in the hall. "Let her speak."

A wave of exclamations swept the room. I swallowed hard, looking at my uncle, whose gaze was no gentler than Wil's. But the fighting had stopped. My friends still lived. I opened my mouth.

"I want to say . . ." The words caught in my throat. There were Wil's black eyes, fixed on me. I would not see him again after tonight, even if I saved him. "I . . . I want to say," I quavered, "that my mother, Lady Æthelflæd, learned from the kings of Wessex—from her father, and then from her brother—to meet her enemies with might and honor. All her life she was a friend and partner to King Edward. Her lands, her wealth, her armies, and even her family she pledged to him." I seized one of Wil's hands and looked back at him with a glare as intense as his own. "Anyone who has ever considered himself an ally of Æthelflæd must understand this. And anyone"—I turned to throw the words back over my shoulder toward Dunstan standing by the door—"who calls himself a friend of Ælfwyn of Mercia must understand it, too. Anyone in this room"—now I made the words ring out through the entire hall—"who says they love the lady's daughter, Ælfwyn, but will not swear fealty to Edward of Wessex, should find a new lord or lady to serve. Get out!" I shouted. "There is no place for you here!"

The hall was completely silent as I turned to Edward. I took a step toward him, then another. Suddenly footsteps sounded behind me.

"No!" I exclaimed, whirling to confront Dunstan, who was striding closer and closer. "No, old friend," I whispered. Dunstan stopped in his tracks. Then with a groan he turned and ran, bursting out through the hall doors.

The hall erupted with shouts. I looked back over my shoulder at Wil, frozen where he stood. Please, just leave, I wanted to call out to him. *Take the others and go quickly, before Osgar has time to stop you.* I wished I could tell him I was sorry. *Wil.* Tears started down my face as I forced my eyes away.

"Ælfwyn." The king said my name in a tone I'd heard him use just once before, when he'd tried to leave me with a few words of comfort in my mother's death chamber. King Edward was holding out his hand to me. *All my freedom, my friends . . .* Wil would still be watching—I had to make him go. I took the king's hand in both of mine. Then, desolate, I knelt and touched his fingers with my lips.

22

AWAY

"ÆLFWYN!"

I squeezed a clod of dirt between my fingers. The earth was still dense and wet. Seeds would take hold and send out roots, I thought, if we had enough sun during the next week. I reached for one of the little cloth sacks I'd laid out beside me.

"Ælfwyn! Where are you?"

Bag of seeds in hand, I stood up. "Here, in the garden," I called back.

Around the side of the wooden house with its steep thatched roof Aunt Dove appeared, carrying a basket. She leaned over the fence that stood between the house and the garden where I'd been working. "I thought you might want some of Sister Wulfrun's bread today, with Edith gone, and you alone." She frowned at my faded dress stained with mud at the hem, my dirt-blackened hands, the wimple I'd taken off and hung behind me on the gatepost. "Edith most certainly is away," she said with a little smile. Since Edith had been allowed to join me here at Sceaftesburh, she had fussed over my appearance almost as much as she had when I was a little girl. But Edith was gone to East Anglia now, fretting over Gytha, who would soon bear her first child. "The old wolf's whelp," Edith liked to say in a sour tone, but her face could not entirely hide the pleasure she felt at the coming of her grandchild. She would be gone for half the spring, I expected, and during that time I intended to grow a yardful of early vegetables.

I brushed off my hands and squinted in the direction of the sun where it glowed behind the clouds that covered the sky. It must be a little past midmorning—Aunt Dove would have finished the midday offices, and maybe she could sit down with me for a talk.

"Will you eat with me if I promise to wash before I come inside?" I asked her.

"With that promise, yes, I can stay for a short while," she said, turning to stroll back to the door of my little house.

I shook the loose dirt from my dress. A meal in my house with Aunt Dove. A year ago would I have guessed that, come another spring, I'd still be shut up here at Sceaftesburh, forbidden to venture out of sight of the abbey? With a sigh, I went to dip a few handfuls of water from the trough inside our stable.

There were no horses here now: King Edward had permitted me to come to this cottage outside the abbey walls with the provision that neither I nor any companion who joined me here would keep a horse. When Edith left for East Anglia two days ago, she went in an oxcart sent specially from Wintanceaster—that was the only way for us to come and go. I splashed my cheeks and straightened up, looking at my fingernails. Most of the black had washed away. Hoping my face was clean, too, I headed in.

"I have some news for you," my aunt said as I entered the house and joined her at the table where she'd laid out a few things for us to eat. "This morning I had a visit from Bishop Frithustan." My eyes widened, and I glanced up from the soft cheese into which I'd begun to dip a piece of the new bread. Frithustan? The bishop of Wintanceaster had come here? But I had no opportunity to ask questions. "He began," my aunt was saying testily, "by reminding me that some churchmen continue to argue that all men and women of holy orders must keep entirely apart, that they should never even occupy the same abbey, as the monks and nuns at Sceaftesburh do." My aunt shook her head. "The men and women in my care have separate quarters for sleeping, and do not eat or pray beside each other—that has always been sufficient in the past. And which of them should I turn out? My monk John, who can heal an ox of any injury this side of death? Sister Wulfrun, the baker's widow, who makes this excellent bread?" She brandished the round loaf. "I need every one of my brothers and sisters at Sceaftesburh. Together we do God's work well."

"Did you wave bread at Bishop Frithustan?" I asked, raising an eyebrow.

"No." She scowled, replacing the loaf on the table. "I listened while he gave me other news, which you should hear." Aunt Dove's voice, which had risen with indignation, suddenly grew quiet and serious. "King Rægnald, the bishop tells me, has indeed accepted Edward as his lord, as have all who live in Northumbria—English, Danish, Norse—everyone." She fell silent, looking at me intently to see how I would take the news.

So it was finally well known, this thing I had guessed when I saw Uncle Edward's coin in Cirenceaster. *Everyone north of the Humber, even Rægnald, who calls himself their king.* "Do you think," I said in a soft voice, "that Edward would let me go back to Lunden, now that matters in Northumbria are resolved?"

Aunt Dove's face was sorrowful as she shook her head. "Not to Lunden, dear. You mustn't hope that he will ever consider that." She took one of my hands in hers. "There are still too many people who would use you, he fears, to challenge the West Saxon throne. He might consider marriage for you, to an ally across the sea, perhaps."

"But I have pledged my loyalty to King Edward and Wessex for everyone to see!" I protested. "I have lived here quietly for well over a year, speaking to no one but you and Edith. Will nothing convince him that I am not a threat?"

"Ælfwyn," my aunt said, and it seemed to me that she spoke with some difficulty, "for your own protection, as well as his, he wants you in a safe place. And you have been happy here, haven't you?" She squeezed my hand. "You have had me, and Edith, and your books, and your writing. I'm going to send your poem back to Wintanceaster with Bishop Frithustan," she added. "I told him the king should see it."

"The king doesn't care about poetry," I muttered.

"The bishop will tell the king what I said, and Edward will read your poem," Aunt Dove responded with certainty. "Listen to me, Wyn. I see how your poem honors my sister Æthelflæd. Judith is indeed as valiant and as loyal to her people as we always found Æthelflæd to be. But Ælfwyn, your Judith *worries* about what she has to do. She says, 'Sorely now is my heart heated and my gloomy mind much afflicted with misery.' I find your Judith more like ... more like you, Ælfwyn. You doubt yourself—I see it—but in the face of your fears, you still try. When Edward reads your poem, in Judith he will see Æthelflæd, the sister he trusted all his life. But I hope he will also see Ælfwyn, who has pledged her own fealty to the crown, and ought not ..." She trailed off.

"And ought not be confined against her will," I finished bleakly. I sat, staring at a bit of bread crust in front of me as the pause lengthened. "So Rægnald will remain enthroned at Eoforwic, promising loyalty to King Edward," I spoke at last.

"And the English and Danes and Norse there are satisfied with that?"

"They trust Wessex to keep peace in Northumbria," Aunt Dove answered. "For now, that is enough."

We were both silent after that, until with another sigh Aunt Dove pushed herself back from the table and stood up. "I'm needed in the scriptorium, they tell me, to supervise the new scribes for an hour or two. We have two nuns who are just completing their training here with us, and a brother who has come all the way from Italy to learn the English way of writing and decoration. Men and women working within sight of each other—what would Bishop Frithustan have to say about that?" She rolled her eyes impatiently, then returned her gaze to me. "Will I see you there this afternoon, Ælfwyn?"

"I've spent most of the past year writing in your scriptorium and reading in your library, Aunt Dove," I replied. "Today I'm going to blacken my fingers with dirt instead of ink." She nodded, and together we went to the doorway.

"You'll be in your garden, then?" she asked as we stopped on the threshold.

"I thought I'd walk to that rocky field where we found rosemary growing. I'd like a plant near the house." Aunt Dove nodded and stepped outside. "The bishop will take my poem to the king?" I blurted out before she could go any farther.

"He'll take it"—she reached back and hugged me close to her—"and the king will see that he need not fear Ælfwyn of Mercia."

Following a well-traveled path, I set out that afternoon, going past the wooden buildings of the abbey and out into the partly tilled fields where a few of the holy brothers from Sceaftesburh were plowing. At least I could walk a little distance away from the settlement by myself, which was better than it had been in Wintanceaster, I tried to comfort myself. A year and a half ago, wouldn't I have been more than content to live at some distance from my uncle's court, well supplied with books and the leisure to read them, and free of the threat of marriage to someone chosen by the king? A year and a half ago that would have felt like an escape. Now it did not.

No one was plowing the stony pasture when I reached it, of course—it had never been worth the bother. Early wildflowers waved, white and yellow on their stems. I found a silvery, fragrant rosemary plant small enough that I could dig it out with the wooden trowel I'd brought. I pressed soil around its roots, lifted it onto the cloth I'd brought to wrap it in, and pushed myself up from where I'd been kneeling.

That's when a movement caught my eye. A horseman was riding up to the edge of my field—or were there two of them? No, it was a man on a dark bay leading a packhorse. They were already quite close, and I started to hear the clink of the horses' gear. The rider raised his arm.

"Ho, woman!" He was coming nearer and nearer. I dropped my trowel. "You there! I see the abbey over that way. Will this path lead me to it?" He was reining in his horse now, just a few paces from where I stood. "Answer me, will you?" the man insisted. "Does this path go to Sceaftesburh?"

"Wil," I said.

It *was* Wil. When I spoke he went completely still. His hair and beard were well trimmed again, I saw—not the wild black tangle I remembered from Cirenceaster—but I think I'd have recognized that glower even if he'd shaved and painted himself blue like a northern pagan. Then he slid down from his horse and took three strides to where I stood.

"Why the devil can't I know you when I see you?" he demanded, then broke off, running his eyes over my clothes and hands. "Are you a slave here, Lady?" he exclaimed. "Has Edward rewarded your loyalty so poorly?"

"No, no." His quick anger almost made me smile, although I was trembling with the surprise of seeing him. "I chose a muddy chore for myself today, that's all. I am kept at Sceaftesburh very comfortably."

"*Kept* at Sceaftesburh," he responded. "Yes. I had heard that." He reached out a hand, then let it fall to his side. "I had heard that," he muttered.

"Where . . . what are you doing at Sceaftesburh?" I faltered. "You're headed for the abbey, you said? To see my aunt?"

"To see Abbess Æthelgifu?" Wil snorted. He stepped back a pace. "Your king wouldn't welcome me in this country, Lady. I'm not about to announce my visit to his sister."

"So you came to—to . . ."

"I came to find Widsith, that beggar," Wil said, rubbing his forehead. "You may remember that the last time I saw him was outside Osgar's hall, where I wished him luck for his performance. For a year now I've wanted to know why Widsith thought it was a good idea not to tell me everything he knew about Lady Ælfwyn of Mercia." There was bitterness in his voice, and I hung my head.

"I—I was running. I wasn't sure whom to trust. I thought it might make things worse for you, if you knew."

"And ignorance was much better, of course! I bring every man and weapon I possess to wreak vengeance on the king and force his hand against Rægnald. You step into the hall and lo, my martyred lady is restored! You then remind us why, after all, we should trust King Edward to deal with the trouble in Northumbria in his own way, and I'm left to run with the few who will still follow me, away from Cirenceaster, possessing only what we have in our saddle-bags, wondering how long we have before the king hears who we are, and sets his riders on our track."

"But he had made a treaty with Rægnald already! And I didn't tell Uncle Edward anything about you," I protested desperately. "I promise you, I said nothing!"

"Indeed, no riders followed us," Wil said in a gentler tone.

"I guessed that we had you to thank for that. And you were right. Rægnald had already sworn fealty to Edward, as everyone now knows." The wind was coming up, blowing my dress until it twisted around my legs. Wil kept talking. "I haven't heard tell of any new scop at Sceaftesburh," he said in the same kind voice.

"I don't play or sing here," I mumbled. "Sometimes I write. I finished my English *Judith*. I think it might be a good poem. Aunt Dove—Abbess Æthelgifu, I mean—is sending it to the king."

"And what do you hope will come of that gift?" Wil wanted to know.

"I . . . I hope he will remember me. I hope he will think of my mother's loyalty and service to him," I replied listlessly.

"He should remember *your* loyalty and service," Wil said with force. "If not for you, he would have faced enough re-bellion at Cirenceaster to badly weaken his Mercian claims. And I will say this: Under my guidance Eoforwic still be-longed to the Danes, but thanks to the treaty with Rægnald, Edward rules north of the Humber at last." Wil shook his head wonderingly. "I would not have guessed that it could be so. But you saw it, Lady? How?"

"I only saw the brother whom Lady Æthelflæd had served and trusted all her life, and opposite him a man I had learned to . . . to admire very much. I didn't want either of you to destroy the other," I replied with difficulty. I looked into Wil's face. "Are you still angry with me?"

Wil didn't answer at once, and I couldn't read his expression. "Last month I went into Northumbria, secretly," he spoke at last. "The Norse took farmland from my people after I was driven out, but as I rode through the countryside, I saw Norse and English and Danish settlers beginning to live side by side, to share a few things with each other. There is even talk of the archbishop returning to Eoforwic Minster before the end of this year . . ." He trailed off.

In the plowed field nearest to the pasture where we stood, the monks had halted their oxen and were pointing at the sky. Spring storm rising. Time to stop. Time to take the tools and animals in. One of the brothers was shading his eyes, peering in our direction.

"I think they've seen you," I told Wil. "You'd better not . . ." Why was it so hard for me to say these words? "You'd better not stay."

"I haven't really told you why I came to Sceaftesburh," he said, ignoring what I'd said.

"To question Widsith—isn't that what you said?" I responded uncertainly, but Wil waved dismissively.

"First of all, I came to bring you your horse," he told me.

"My horse?" I turned around to stare at the riderless mount again. "Winter!"

"When his cold-weather coat started to grow in—all those long white hairs coming through the dun—it took a month for me to figure out what you'd done." Winter was still softly mottled with brown and dirty from traveling. I rubbed his arched neck.

"Thank you. But I can't keep a horse at Sceaftesburh," I said. "The king won't allow . . ." I glanced over my shoulder again—now all of the monks were staring at us. "Wil, in another moment they'll be coming. You—you can't stay here, talking like this. You've got to leave now!"

"I don't intend to leave Winter with you at Sceaftesburh," Wil said, gazing at me.

"You don't?" One of the brothers had begun walking toward us.

"I brought your horse for you to ride," Wil said, his eyes fixed on my face, "away from Sceaftesburh, west, and then north, with me." Now I was staring back at him. "There is a little church," Wil was saying quickly, "in the Welsh mountains, where almost no one goes except the priest who comes to pray with the half-pagan folk there. A few—only a few—of the people in the village know anything about the stranger who has come to live in the stone house just outside the churchyard. Mostly they don't ask questions." He drew a breath. "You could come with me, Ælfwyn. I have the house, some land, and there are a few men who work my fields. Some of our friends have come to live nearby, establishing their own holdings. Kenelm is one who has found a place among the Welsh—I see him sometimes—and Dunstan may be coming. It's green and cool there beside the mountain chapel." The words tumbled out of him now. "The fields follow the curve of the hills. There's a stand of beech-wood just beyond my house—tall, graceful trees . . ." His voice trailed off.

When Wil spoke again his voice was very soft, and his breath warmed my cheek as he leaned close to say, "I learned a poem once, written as if a scop were telling stories in his own voice. In one tale he sang about how two lovers, a noble man and woman, could think of nothing but each other, until love reft them of all sleep. I have thought of you, Ælfwyn of Mercia," Wil whispered, "until I am reft of all sleep."

I know that poem, I wanted to tell him. *Mother taught me to hear the scop's voice in those words written so perfectly on parchment, to think of a singer and an audience, not just letters in straight lines.* Deor is the scop's name, I opened my lips to say.

And instead I kissed him, tangling my muddy fingers in his dark hair.

"They're coming, Lady," Wil said when I let him go.

I was already hauling myself onto Winter's back, tugging at his lead rope to turn his head westward, certain as we lifted into a gallop that Wil would be right behind me.

"So," THE LADY FINISHED, CRADLING HER CHILD IN THE FIRE-light, "as our visitor said, it is written in the Mercian Chronicle that the winter after Lady Æthelflæd's death her daughter, Ælfwyn, was bereft of all authority among the Mercians, and taken by King Edward into Wessex. No other mention of Ælfwyn appears in Mercia's Chronicle, nor in any West Saxon history.

"But listen: Once a traveler, unwelcome where she'd been born, found a resting place in the mountains where the Welsh kings rule. The man who brought her there was an honorable lord—he cared for his lands and his household, fought when he had to, and the two of them lived quietly in that green place.

"And any mountain wanderer who asks to pass the night with this lady and lord will find a pleasing welcome. The visitor's mount, if he has one, is turned out to pasture with an old white warhorse who, the lady will mention, learned to pull a plow, but now grows lazier and rounder each day with his nose buried in the hillside grass. Inside the villa the guest will have a place near the fire, good food, a comfortable chair. The lord and lady will ask him where he has been and what he has seen. If he has a tale to tell, they will gladly hear it, and reward him with a gift or a coin for the telling.

"But if the traveler sits mute and weary, the lady herself may take up her harp. She knows the story of a captured princess, and a tale of separated lovers. She can sing the lament of a scop who lost the favor of his king. She will watch the listener consider these misfortunes alongside his own. And she will know what to say to ease the pain of whatever he has lost.

"That passed away. So may this."

Historical Note

Sometimes history leaves you hanging. At the height of her powers Æthelflæd, Lady of the Mercians, suddenly died. Did her only daughter, Ælfwyn, mourn her mother's death? Did she expect to rule Mercia after Æthelflæd? The Anglo-Saxon Chronicles don't tell us, nor do they mention Ælfwyn again after her uncle Edward, the West Saxon king, removes her from Mercia a few months later. Ælfwyn simply disappears.

What might have happened to her? When I looked at some of the roles open to Anglo-Saxon noblewomen, I was hard pressed to decide. Ælfwyn might have been a *freothuwebbe*—a peace weaver—strengthening an alliance through her marriage. Or she might have become a nun, fully committed to the church and her religious vows. Did she inherit land, and have to manage an estate and tenants? In light of her family's famous dedication to reading and education, it seemed likely that Ælfwyn knew how to read and write—maybe she even translated and composed poetry like her grandfather Alfred.

Maybe . . . but all the historical record can offer is a sigh of regret for this orphaned and dispossessed child of a famous leader. It made me think: Some Anglo-Saxon poet, some scop, ought to have composed tragic lines in memory of Ælfwyn. In Old English literature some of the most melancholy voices belong to wandering scops who lament the loss of their homes and loved ones. Ælfwyn's case reminded me of older stories in poems like *Deor, Beowulf,* or *Wulf and Eadwacer,* where noble heirs fall prey to the ambitions of their relatives. A scop might have shaped Ælfwyn's tale into verses, and then sung them in Mercian feasting halls.

The idea of letting Ælfwyn herself become such a scop interested me for several reasons. A few Old English poems seem like they might be spoken by a woman's voice. And we know there were literate women in Anglo-Saxon society who valued poetry: Saint Hild of Whitby, the greatest British abbess, nurtured the talents of Cædmon, whose creation poem remains one of the most important compositions in English.

But most important for my story, Ælfwyn the scop and writer would be able to speak on her own behalf. An Anglo-Saxon carving may show you what one of their ships looked like, but it doesn't communicate how it felt to sail on such a vessel. On the other hand, when the speaker of the Old English poem we call *The Seafarer* says, "My soul amid the sea-flood wanders wide over the whales' land," we catch a vivid glimpse of his experience of a sea voyage, just for a moment. What I craved for Ælfwyn was a voice like these ancient poetic ones I sometimes encounter in Old English writing. At last, I thought, she'd have a chance to tell us how it felt to be Lady Æthelflæd's daughter, and then to lose her, and to carry on afterward. Who could do that better than a scop?